AF268398

DEAD THINGS GROW HERE

Content Warning

This novel contains themes and scenes that some readers may find distressing, including:

- Grief and loss
- Suicide and its aftermath
- Mental health struggles
- Psychological trauma
- Descriptions of violence and body horror

Reader discretion is advised. If you are sensitive to any of these topics, please take care while reading.

If you or someone you know is struggling, consider reaching out to a mental health professional or support service.

For those who hear a noise outside their window at night and think 'it's just the wind'… this is for you.

Prologue

Professor Anderson

I woke with a jolt as the sun was setting, casting golden beams through the crack in the curtains. The room was colder, the air heavier. Had I really slept all day, or was it a trick of the light again? I gave myself a minute to lie there and reassess my decision not to grab my belongings and head out the door this morning, knowing I should have gone whilst there had been the opportunity. Why hadn't I? Leaving just wasn't something I could bring myself to do.

I recalled my dream as nausea swam up my chest. There had to be an explanation for all of this. Perhaps everything that happened was a dream, or a hallucination. Stress. Maybe the mould in the cabin walls is affecting my brain chemistry.

I sat up and took deep breaths to steady my breathing; giving myself a panic attack now wouldn't help me.

Dragging myself up, I rubbed my eyes and stretched out my now even tighter muscles. I shuffled down the corridor and into the living room. The sun through the curtains hit me as I squinted to see my surroundings. I slumped in the hard wooden chair and took deep breaths to clear my head.

I felt warm droplets hit my hands. Glancing down, I saw the crimson droplets growing faster. Reaching for my nose, I pinched it and ran to the bathroom.

The shower hissed as the freezing water escaped the pipes, making me jump at the sudden break of silence. The ice-cold water hit my body, causing me to shiver as if I'd fallen into a bath of needles. I let the water wash over my body as it heated. The blood came off my hands and face, vanishing entirely, save for the pressure on my nose. A nosebleed hadn't occurred since the day I lost my wife. Stress used to always cause them. I forced myself to relax. The heat soothed my tight muscles, and the feeling of tension and unease began to wash away.

I breathed slower.

I was lucky, wasn't I? Not everyone gets an opportunity like this. Space. Quiet. A secluded place to do my research and unravel my mind. Maybe I had unravelled it too far.

I smiled as I slathered the rose-scented soap all over my body. I felt calmer and steadier now. Perhaps I imagined what I saw. What I thought I saw.

Maybe last night had all been a very intense dream. Paranoia triggered by isolation.

Maybe.

I'm a practical man; I always have been. I have been interested in science my whole life. My father was a professor at the same university that I worked at now, and his grandfather before him. It ran in my blood, the curiosity about the universe. How things worked, how they existed, and why they failed to exist any longer.

Now, standing here as the warm water flushed away my anxiety, I wondered if I'm giving up too easily. Maybe I need to see it one more time. Just once more. Then I will leave.

Curiosity did kill the cat after all, and I was no longer sure I had nine lives left to spend.

I stepped out of the shower and wrapped an old towel around myself. The drain gurgled behind me, swallowing the last of my comfort. The rumbling of my stomach distracted me from my thoughts, forcing me to realise I needed to eat. When did I last eat? The days had seemed to blur. I looked over towards the mirror and jumped; I wasn't expecting to see the blurred reflection of myself, and it startled me. I could barely make out the reflection of myself standing there through the thick steam and without my glasses, probably for the best. As I reached for my glasses, I quietly cursed, remembering I'd forgotten the extractor. It was so steamy in there that I couldn't see out of them. Typical. I would not shower with the windows open, not after last night.

Not here.

I wiped my glasses with the edge of the towel as I made my way through the steam-filled room toward the window. I reached above the frame and clicked the button for the extractor. As I pulled my arm down, a gust of cold air came over me, like a door left open on a cold winter's morning.

My body stiffened.

There were no windows or doors open; that much I had checked. I glanced down at the window latch. No, still shut. A waft of earth-filled air travelled up my nostrils.

I turned my head up to look out of the window in front of me. My heart froze. My eyes locked on the window. There it was. Standing right on the other side. Or was it *in* the window? I didn't know. I caught my breath and stared at myself.

A reflection of myself, yes. The same grey-streaked, short black hair. My beard, thicker than I liked. The ever-more apparent crow's feet at the sides of my eyes and frown lines on my forehead. My stone-cold brown eyes. The big, wide, haunting smile that was plastered across my face. It looked exactly like me. But it couldn't be me.

Because I wasn't smiling.

That smile that didn't belong on a human face. The wide grin stretched inhumanly high up to my cheekbones, revealing a thick row of teeth. So many teeth.

It didn't move. It didn't blink. Its eyes didn't even seem wet. Its breath didn't fog the glass. My chest rose and fell with my staggered breath, but the thing in the window didn't move at all.

I parted my mouth to speak. I wanted to know what it wanted, what it was doing, who it was, but no words escaped. My body became completely frozen.

Was this real?

I stumbled back in shock and disgust at what stared back at me. My reflection didn't move; it stayed grinning at me, mocking me in my terror. My foot slipped in the motion, slamming back onto the floor, narrowly missing the towel hook on the wall. I thumped the back of my head against the cold, slippery tiles. Pain shot through my skull and down my spine. Dazed and dizzy, I groaned. I tried to stand, but my legs deceived me. Clawing at the wet floor, I pulled myself onto my front and dragged myself out of the bathroom.

Get up. Move. Now.

In a snake-like motion, I dragged myself through the living room until I reached the table and pulled myself up in a panicked, jerking motion. I could have sworn I could hear low, sinister laughter coming from the bathroom. Heart pounding and hands shaking, I opened my laptop. My hands trembled as I typed.

I needed to reach Amelia. I needed to warn her. Whatever was happening out here, she couldn't be a part of it. I remembered the way she looked that day in the lab, eyes wide with fascination, explaining her findings. I couldn't let the same curiosity lead her here. This had gone too far. I should never have invited her. This place was no longer safe. Whatever it was, it had seen me. And worse, it had wanted *me* to see *it*.

My vision blurred in and out; the screen was swimming before me. Each breath became harder to take than the last. My fingers moved sluggishly across the keyboard; they weren't listening to my commands. My skin was ice-cold again, my limbs beginning to numb.

The cursor blinked on the screen as I finished typing the sentence. With a last burst of effort, I hit send.

Everything tilted.

My knees buckled. My vision wasn't mine to control anymore.

As my vision faded, the tapping began again. Slow. Rhythmic. Right up against the window.

And I collapsed onto the hard wooden floor. Silence filled the cabin once more.

I could barely remember why I was on the floor when I first woke up. My skull throbbed with a pounding rhythm, each beat crashing like waves against the shore of my mind. Blurred light trickled through the cabin slats. My vision was patchy; the edges grey and ghost-like. I blinked hard, trying to recall how I had ended up here. My hand instinctively reached behind my head. Pain flared instantly. When I pulled my hand back, crimson smeared across my fingers.

Warm. Sticky. Too much. It instantly grounded me. I'd blacked out.

My heart rate rose and panic flooded my chest. As I tried to stand, a nauseating wave crashed through me. The room spun. The walls bent inwards. The ceiling expanded. Everything felt unfamiliar and too close, as if someone had trapped me inside a snow globe and wouldn't stop shaking it. I threw on my clothes, instinctively shoving my torch into my pocket, and stumbled to the front door, flinging it open for air, not even bothering to grab a coat. The cold punched me in the chest, and the storm outside screamed in my ears.

Reality caught up.

The air smelled of wet bark and something else: decay? No. Not quite. It was the scent of something left too long in the dark.

Rain stabbed at my skin like needles, but I barely noticed. All I could think about was the last few days. The reflection. The footprints. The feeling of being watched. Of not being alone.

My bare feet crunched against the old wooden porch as I turned my head toward the ground. I didn't want to look. But I had to. The footprints flashed in my mind. I hoped they would not be there. I knew they would be.

Of course, they were.

Fresh. Wet. Sunken deep into the mud before the edge of the cabin. They led around it, carving an arc from the porch window to the bathroom, right where I had seen it last.

I didn't need to follow them; I knew where they would stop. And where they would disappear.

I stood there, just staring at the footprints.

The wind howled louder now, almost sentient, almost laughing. The rain, once steady, now fell in broken rhythms, throwing off the beat of my sanity. My breath came in tight, shallow waves. I focused on the sound of the branches rattling in the wind. Focused on the slosh of water puddling around my feet. Anything to keep my mind tethered. Anything to remind me this was real. This was real.

Except… it wasn't. Not completely.

Because now the lake was calling me again.

The reflection.

My mind flicked back to earlier. The reflection in the window, it had watched me.

That smile. That dead-eyed stare. The face that was mine, but not.

Reflections had always fascinated me. Mirrors in particular. As a scientist, I appreciated the physics of light. The way reflection and refraction worked. But lately, mirrors hadn't just become reflections. Reflections became portals to something that defied physics.

A cold coiled around my stomach.

I wanted to smash every reflective surface around the cabin. But I knew better. If I smashed the windows, it could get in. It could find me.

Had it always been watching? Waiting?

I didn't believe in ghosts, or aliens, or alternate universes. But here I was, getting hunted by my own reflection.

Suddenly, there was something else. A sound. Not thunder, or rain or even the wind. Something else. It was a voice. Muffled and distant. I couldn't quite work out what it was saying. I was alone, I reminded myself; I was out here *alone*.

I strained to hear it. The sound was muffled at first but then grew louder and more demanding. My heartbeat pounded in my ears. It wasn't calling to me. It was calling like me. Imitating me.

I staggered backwards, almost slipping on the wet porch, but steadied myself on the door frame.

A second voice? This one sounded female.

"Darling?" I called.

No…it couldn't be. It wasn't her.

I couldn't shake the intense feeling that I needed to find out. An urgency that consumed me.

The thunder and wind came back into focus as if someone had just turned up the volume of the storm.

Had I imagined it? Was it bait? There it was again.

Definitely a female voice.

"Help me…"

Like a dream filtered through static.

Leaving my front door wide open, I stepped off the porch into the full force of the rain.

The storm swallowed me instantly. The voice was captivating, and its call was clear — it needed help.

Instinctively, I walked forward towards the calls, stopping for a brief second to pick a lone pink tulip before I continued. I couldn't see her again empty-handed. Even though I could barely see, something urged me onward. I didn't know if it was hope or madness. Maybe both.

I continued in my trance-like state. Branches clawed at my arms like skeletal fingers. Roots reached up from the soil as if to grab my ankles, trying to trip me each step I took. My body moved on instinct. It knew the way.

The further I walked into the forest, the quieter the storm became.

The world quietened until all I could hear was my heartbeat. And her voice.

The sky was raven-black with only a trickle of silver speckles. With the combination of darkness and the blanket of rain, I couldn't see where I was going at all. But I knew. I could just feel it. Mechanically stepping over each rock and weaving in and out of the labyrinth of trees, it was as if I had walked this route every day for my entire life. The sky contorted into ribbons of black and gold as lightning struck overhead. The damp, decaying air flew around me, but I proceeded up the path. The calls got louder and more intense.

I walked faster. Then I stopped. I knew where I was now.

Still. Wide. Black.

The moonlight bled across the lake's surface; its maker hung as the centrepiece in the sky.

My visibility was low, but the light of the moon gave me some slight shadows to work with. I looked around me, searching for the woman, scanning the edge of the lake for a shadow.

Nothing.

But I knew she wouldn't be at the edge of the lake. I knew where I needed to look.

I shuffled past the scattered tulips growing along the edge of the clearing and around the lake, as if they were guiding my path.

When I was finally at its bank, I stopped, and I knelt.

The dirt was soft, almost too soft, like stretched skin over a trampoline.

The lake had never looked so calm. So inviting. I no longer felt any fear, like a vessel fulfilling its programmed task. I don't think I had ever felt this calm before.

There was something eerily peaceful about the lake's aura. I felt as though I could stay here for hours.

But the voice. She needed my help.

Slowly, I turned my head to look at the surface of the lake. Mesmerised by what I was seeing, I stared deeper and deeper into the dark abyss. Swirls of shimmery pinks and purples danced hand in hand with the obsidian black water. The colours laced in and out of each other like a bowl full of snakes. The beauty of it felt... wrong. Too perfect. Like something that wanted to be seen.

I noticed the colours beginning to part and the black took centre stage.

Then, there it was. My reflection. It stared at me with gleeful malice. Its eyes wide and unblinking. It copied my movements. Slowly and exactly. Then, it stopped. My hands shook; my breath staggered. It was here. In front of me. And all I could do was stare at it.

I'd spent years outrunning the things I couldn't name. But they had names now. My reflection gave them form. And it wanted me to see them. Its smile widened before mine did. Then it stopped mirroring me altogether.

"Come closer."

It spoke without words. I stopped, just for a second. My body leaned forward, but my mind screamed for me to pull back.

This isn't right.

Every instinct begged me to run, to turn away, to break whatever spell the lake had cast. But my legs wouldn't move.

The reflection's grin widened, its eyes locked onto mine like a predator watching prey accept its fate. And in that moment, the fear didn't matter anymore. I fought the feeling. My hands trembled. My breath caught in my throat.

This isn't right.

The lake pulsed beneath me like it was alive, like it had been waiting for this. My body swayed closer again. The voice returned, soft this time, coaxing. Something inside me screamed, *Move. Run.* But it was too late. I had already crossed the edge of resistance.

And then, my body tipped forward. Like a puppet giving in to the strings. The colours in the lake became completely engulfed in black. It defied every principle. It couldn't be me. It can't-

Suddenly a hand flew towards me, causing me to fall to the floor, which would have hurt if I weren't so full of shock.

Long. Bone-white. Fingers stretched beyond what human bones should allow.

I screamed, and the trees shuddered in sympathy.

The hand latched onto my ankle; claws ripping through my flesh as I tried to pull away.

They dug deep.

My blood oozed over the bony fingers and seeped into the ground. Its grasp grew tighter.

I clawed at the grainy dirt as I tried to free myself from the grasp. The soil packed beneath my nails, mixing with blood. The stench of iron and rot hit my nose, making me gag and I fought to get away. The hand pulled me closer and closer towards the lake.

I let out another cry as a second hand erupted from the water, gripping my right arm. As its claws dug into my humerus, it yanked my arm back in one abrupt motion. With a sickening pop, my shoulder ripped out of its socket.

Pain split my chest like lightning.

My mind screamed that this wasn't real. My body knew better.

I clawed at the earth with my one free arm, nails tearing through the grit and soil. Every kick and lurch was met with stronger resistance.

Nothing I did seemed to faze it as it submerged my lower half into the lake.

I turned my body towards the abyss, letting go of all instincts to get away. I relaxed my body into the inevitable.

The lake bubbled. The fear had passed. I knew what awaited.

My reflection emerged from the surface like a corpse.

The skin was bloated and pale. The eyes were glassy, void of light. Its lips peeled back into the same awful grin.

It looked deep into my eyes. I could barely recognise my own reflection anymore. It was as if all of my dark thoughts, all the sins I had ever committed, personified into a living reflection of myself.

Then, it tilted its head. The reflection's face peeled back in layers. Its jawline flapped open like torn paper. Beneath it, something else grinned.

The last thing I saw was my own face stretched into something monstrous.

All my sins. All my thoughts. Everything I had tried to hide.

And then… darkness.

A hollow, sucking sound filled the air as its short, pointy teeth clasped over my head and around my throat. Skinning my face in rings, as if unwrapping meat from bone. It sucked the remaining bloody pulp from where my face once was.

With one last crash, it pulled the lifeless body into the water and disappeared.

Only silence remained. Silence and Anderson's small hand torch, which lay abandoned by the side of the lake. The torch flickered once. Then nothing. Not even ripples disturbed the lake's surface. It was as if he'd never existed at all.

Chapter 1

Lucas

When I first laid eyes on Amelia, I could have sworn I knew her from another life. I had never felt so drawn to someone before. She was the most familiar stranger.

She was moving into another dorm after hers had been temporarily closed because of water damage: too much rain, too little funding, and a roof too old and too damaged. Trying to juggle too many boxes at once, she lost her grip, sending everything crashing to the concrete. I ran to help. She thanked me as we knelt to divide the contents of the split box between the remaining two.

And then she looked up. With wide, doe-like eyes and a crooked smile that would soon become my undoing, I just knew. In that moment, something shifted. We were meant to be part of each other's lives.

That was two years ago. Now, I was here. In the dusty, worn-out university library. Watching her. Reminiscing about the first time we met and how I still feel the exact same way about her.

She stood just behind the rows of towering bookshelves, stacking more research papers. The light caught in her chocolate-brown hair, tinting it almost amber. The low lighting in the library gave everything a golden glow, like candlelight. Almost romantic.

She stood on her tiptoes to reach one of the papers on the top shelf, too stubborn to grab the ladder and too focused to care. Her concentration made her oblivious, but not to me. I watched as she brushed a strand of hair behind her ear, her lips moving slightly as she read the title of a paper. She was beautiful. Captivating.

Dust swirled around me, mixed with the musty scent of old books, causing me to cough suddenly, tears brimming my eyes. Sitting in this time capsule of a place wasn't my idea of a good time. But she was here—so I was, too.

It was all because of her. My reason for staying late in the library. My reason was getting up early to beat the freshman rush at the coffee shop. My reason for staying in university instead of dropping out, like I wanted to, after my mum's death. She was always my reason.

"Lucas! I've found it!" she whispered, loudly enough that she may as well have just spoken.

Her voice shot straight through me and snapped me out of my thoughts. My cheeks grew hot, and I glanced down and pretended to read the book on the desk in front of me. Running my hand through my mousy blonde hair, which was overdue for a haircut, I looked up and smiled as she bounded towards me. All her energy and excitement reminding me of how my old cocker spaniel used to greet me at the door.

"Are you sure that's definitely it?" I asked, squinting as I tried to read the cover of the book she waved in front of me.

That's what I was hoping for. Dull academic journals had bored me enough for one night.

Amelia frowned. "Of course, I'm sure. I'm the one who found it." Her frown curled into a smug smile. Modesty had never been her strongest quality.

"Okay, great!" I replied, perhaps with a little too much enthusiasm. "We'll look at it tomorrow, but let's go to bed. I'm exhausted. I'll walk you back first."

How intently I had been watching her earlier made me feel a little embarrassed. I hoped she hadn't noticed.

"Lucas, you're joking, right?" She rolled her eyes with exaggerated flair. "We've been looking for this for hours. Now you want to leave?"

Disappointment filled her eyes. I knew how excited she was to find this paper, but it was nearly two in the morning, and we both had early lectures.

"I promise you, Mils, we will look at it. We both need some sleep. We can go through it tomorrow, all night if you want to."

With tomorrow being Friday and neither of us going home for the weekend or the autumn break next week, I knew we had plenty of time.

"Yeah, I guess you're right," she admitted. "But promise me you won't forget tomorrow?"

I smiled. Partly at the thought of leaving the library, mostly at the thought of an entire weekend with her. I began packing my bag. There was no way I'd forget to spend an entire night with Amelia, even if it was just to look through some old research paper.

"I promise. I won't forget," I said, flashing her a smile.

As we stepped outside, the October air had turned noticeably colder. It circled around us like a pack of wolves, and I was glad I had remembered my jacket this time.

The Imperial College in London is an incredible university. With their renowned environmental economics course and it being only a forty-five-minute journey from home, it was ideal. Not that I visited home much, there wasn't much left for me in Essex anymore. But when the weather turned like this, I sometimes wished I had studied abroad. Somewhere warmer.

Sometimes, I questioned why I had chosen this course. I had always wanted to be a vet, but being a vet meant getting a lot of good grades in college. It also meant nearly seven years of studying. I figured with this course I could make a difference in the wild instead; change some habitats, work with wild animals. I wasn't too sure, but it felt right when I saw it. Now, walking out the door with Amelia next to me whilst she clutched her books and spoke enthusiastically about climate change, it made me think whether the universe had planned for me to do this course for an entirely different reason.

The pathway was quiet and dimly lit. No one else was around at this time of night. A low fog hung overhead, making the streetlights resemble a blanket of orange-tinted snow. No stars, no moon — not in the middle of London. There was too much light pollution for that, even on a clear night. The air smelled damp and cool. It was going to rain tonight.

I looked down at Amelia, who was still deep into her explanation, and noticed she was shivering. As brilliant as she was, her outfit preparation wasn't always the most practical. I took off my jacket and draped it over her shoulders. She looked up at me and smiled, one cheek dimpled slightly deeper than the other.

"Thank you," she said, her signature smile lighting up her face. "But now you're going to be cold, and this looks more like a dress on me, anyway." She shrugged the jacket off her delicate shoulders and handed it back to me.

"No, honestly, I'm fine. We're nearly there." I took the jacket and placed it back over her.

She was stubborn, but even she wouldn't deny warmth in this weather twice.

We walked in silence for a while, both knowing the dorm was a ten-minute walk away, but neither of us minding the quiet. Amelia twirled her hair around her finger, I noticed as the movements quickened. She always did this when she was anxious or had something on her mind. She would be bald if she carried on. I touched her wrist as we walked. She looked up at me, dropping the curl of hair from her fingers.

"Oh, I forgot to tell you, I emailed him again today." Her voice broke the quiet.

She looked at me with excitement, almost missing the start of the stairs as she hopped up them.

I raised an eyebrow. "What? Professor Anderson?"

I didn't know why I felt like this, but a wave of jealous washed over me. I tried to mask my expression.

"No, the pope. Yes, of course. Professor Anderson!" She rolled her eyes.

I let out a small laugh. Humour might not have been one of her strong suits, but she still made me laugh.

"What did he say?" I was questioning why a professor who wasn't even currently at the university would be so eagerly emailing a student.

"Nothing. He hasn't answered me yet," she said, still looking ahead.

Her words were matter of fact but the way her voice cracked… she was upset. I scrunched up my face, unable to mask all my emotions.

"Right. Then why don't you just find another professor to help you with your dissertation?"

I didn't mean for my words to sound so harsh, but my jealousy was seeping through them.

"Don't be like that." She nudged my arm with her shoulder as we walked. "You know how much he could help my work. It would be stupid not to try again. You know Professor Anderson. He's been our lecturer for the past two years. He just wants to help."

I tried to hide my growing annoyance now, but it bubbled beneath the surface. "I know. It's just weird. I get that he offered his help last year, but a lot has happened since then. Leave the guy alone and ask someone else?"

Something in her eyes changed. They were bright before, now they flushed with something darker. The redder her cheeks became, the quicker her eyes filled with tears.

"Don't speak to me like that!" she said.

She stopped in her place and turned away from me, wiping her eyes. I stood for a moment, contemplating my next move. I hadn't meant to make her upset; I just wanted her to see some perspective. Before I could choose my next move, she turned forward and continued walking up the path, drawing a deep breath the steady herself.

"I understand where you're coming from, but you don't understand. We discussed a lot before summer. He was really helping me. We brainstormed so many topics before coming up with my dissertation. The effect of climate change on the UK's food security was perfect. He helped me come up with it, so only he can help me."

I loved the way she lit up when she talked about her work. Or anything, really. She reminded me of my mum when she used to show off her new paintings, eyes bright with hope. The feeling scared me. She was so similar. Every time I looked at Amelia, I could see a subtle glimpse of my mum in her eyes.

She was so caring. I was all about helping animals. Amelia? She was all about helping other people.

I realised I had become lost in my thoughts and hadn't answered her. Her passion overwhelmed me. I just watched her; her brown eyes glowing under the streetlights looked like caramel chocolate. I'd always had a sweet tooth. She twirled her hair between her fingers again. I smiled and pulled her into me as I walked her the rest of the way to her dorm.

I thought about her during the entire walk back to my room. If there was anything more between her and Anderson other than a professional relationship, she'd tell me, right?

Perhaps the professor was just helping her with her dissertation. She was brilliant. Any professor would be lucky to help her.

I tried to push my thoughts of Amelia and focus on tomorrow. It was already late. I knew I was unlikely to sleep.

As I approached the grey typical London entrance to my dorm, a rustling sound pulled me from my thoughts.

The small, browning bushes whispered in the wind, but there was something else. There was something *in* them. I rarely saw any animals on this side of campus, especially with the continuous construction on the old dorm block next door. A fox, maybe? No, I'd have seen a fox through the leaves. A rat? It could be a rat. As I inched closer to the bushes, seriously considering why I didn't just walk in the door and forget about it, the rustling grew louder.

My stomach twinged with a sudden bout of panic. If it were a rat, maybe it'd jump out and bite me. At least I could skip lectures. I took a deep breath and took another step closer.

The wind picked up, howling. Goosebumps crawled up my arms like a thousand ice-cold spiders. I shivered and stopped. What was I doing?

I turned back towards the door of my dorm. Silence.

No more wind blew. The cars. The world. Everything was still. The world was holding its breath. I slowly looked down.

A small flurry of feathers whisked past me, so close to my face I could feel the wind from its wings. I jumped at the sudden movement, tripping over myself and landing with a hard thump on my back. The fall knocked all the breath out of my lungs. The small ball landed on the bush behind me. I turned my body towards it to get a better look. The tiny robin stared back at me, head twitching from side to side as if it were mimicking my movements. I caught my breath, laughing nervously as I pulled myself to my feet.

My mum had always told me that when robins visited, it was a good omen. She used to tell me my nan had visited us from 'the other side' when a little robin perched on our windowsill.

"Hi, Mum," I said, a sad smile reaching my cheeks.

I gave the bird a wave. It twitched its head once more to the other side.

I shook myself out of it. Glancing around me, I quickly disappeared into my dorm before anyone could see me attempting to be the next *Dr. Dolittle.*

I tossed and turned all night; I just couldn't sleep. I couldn't get the thought of her out of my head. Well, her and Professor Anderson. My mind just wouldn't shut off. I ended up giving up on my attempt to sleep and stuck one of my favourite horror movies on, *Nightmare on Elm Street,* until I eventually, mercifully, drifted off to sleep just as the sun was rising.

Chapter 2

Amelia

Two missed calls, three texts and a voice note. I wasn't sure why Lucas was ignoring me, and the fact he hadn't turned up to class was worrying. Did I upset him yesterday? I knew I probably shouldn't have told him about emailing Anderson. As innocent as it was, I had just been looking for some guidance and support for my dissertation. But I knew Lucas didn't see it that way. Why was he overly protective towards me? And if he was reacting like this to the emails, I couldn't imagine how he would respond when I told him what I was thinking of doing during the autumn break.

My palms became tacky, and my thoughts spiralled. A few of my classmates turned around and gave me dirty looks for my irritating foot tapping that I hadn't realised I was doing.

I slowed my legs still and twirled my dark hair around my fingers as I tried to focus on Dr. Thorton's lecture. I loved my course, but Thorton's endless drone about the effects of climate change on endangered species and how that would subsequently end up killing us and the economy (or something along those lines) wasn't quite doing it for me today.

Suddenly, the door crashed open, banging against the wall. The old hinges were giving way, and I'm sure they wouldn't last much longer, not after that. Lucas threw Thorton an apologetic wave and hurried up the steps, sliding into the seat next to me. Thorton cleared his throat and continued to drone on, clearly unimpressed with Lucas's tardiness or his dramatic entrance.

He didn't look at me as he opened his bag and sorted through his books to find the right one. A wave of awkwardness washed over me. He'd never acted this elusively before. Why did he care so much about the professor? Was he really that jealous?

There was nothing to be jealous of. My stomach fluttered and my cheeks grew warmer when I realised that I had just been staring at him and hadn't even said a word yet.

"Did you not get my messages?" I studied his face, his messy blonde hair falling over his tired blue eyes. He definitely hadn't showered this morning.

"Yes. And your voice note. And your missed calls." Lucas's tone was short. He was still upset.

"I'm sorry. It's not like you to be late. I was worri--"

"Can we all focus on the lesson?" Thorton interrupted, barking from the front.

I felt the heat rise in my cheeks. I wasn't used to being in a teacher's bad books, and now the entire class had turned to stare.

Sensing my discomfort, Lucas grabbed my hand and flashed me a cheeky smile.

At least he was smiling. Maybe he wasn't *that* mad.

We always took a walk in Hyde Park during our two-hour break between lectures. I usually enjoy the peace of nature. Squirrels darting up the dense trees, an unleashed terrier barking furiously as if today might be the day it caught one. Pigeons fought over someone's leftover sandwich, and ducks glided across the pond, occasionally dipping their heads below the water. When I was little, my mum would tell me they were checking to see if they were wearing pants. The memory made me smile to myself as we walked along the promenade.

I loved our walks together. It was often the highlight of my day.

Today, though, we walked in a tension-filled silence.

"I'm sorry," Lucas said at last. "I couldn't sleep last night, and when I finally did, I slept through my alarm."

He tore off a piece of his baguette and tossed it over to a pigeon, prompting a dozen more to swoop down and squabble over the treat.

"That's okay. I just… you know." I looked up into his deep blue eyes. If the ponds at this park were the same colour, I'd never leave. He was classically handsome. Just over 6 feet tall, with a strong jawline and a smile to complement it. He worked out, so he had a good physique too. It was a shame he didn't seem to see these things in himself.

"I wouldn't have wanted you to miss out on one of Thorton's riveting lectures," I added with a cheeky grin, hoping it would be reciprocated.

It wasn't. Instead, he stopped and sat on a damp wooden bench beside the pond. It had rained last night, and the smell of wet grass filled the air. Sitting next to him, I gently grabbed his hand.

"I had a lot on my mind." He mumbled.

I let go of his hand and rolled my eyes. Would he ever get over this? It wasn't like we were getting married and having kids, we sent a few emails to each other!

"Are you jealous of me asking a professor to help with my dissertation?" I blurted.

My annoyance finally boiled over. Closing my eyes, I waited for his response, but no response came. I drew in a deep breath and tried to rescue the conversation. "I wanted to talk about this with you last night, but you didn't want to. I want to go through some of the old emails between me and Prof. Anderson. They're… off."

I had thought little of it at the time when I received the emails. I put it down to Anderson's quirky personality, but with him not answering my last few emails, I couldn't help but look a little deeper into their meaning. It worried me that he was in that cabin all on his own. He told me it was very remote, which made me worry about his mental state out there. Being alone wasn't good for anybody's mental health. When he told me where it was, I looked it up. He was right, it was about a 30-minute drive off any main road in Scotland, up some dirt tracks and semi-made roads. But it looked beautiful from the few old pictures I could find. Small, but beautiful. In some of the first few emails he sent to me whilst he was out there, he mentioned how he would have loved to have had the time to take his wife out there, but his work always took over. Apparently, she would have loved it. He stopped talking about her after a while. Actually, he stopped talking about much of anything at all. He bought the cabin for them for their ten-year wedding anniversary. That's all he said to me. He said nothing else, but I assumed he went up there after she died as a kind of homage to her.

Lucas scoffed. He didn't respond. He just continued to stare at the floor, tearing off pieces of his baguette.

"Not like that. Not how you're thinking. Look." I reached into my bag and pulled out my laptop.

I passed it over to him. "Look, start with this one. He sent it around a month ago, just after I first emailed him about my dissertation."

Lucas looked at the screen.

Dear Amelia,

I will happily help you with any information you need. I'd be happy to talk through any ideas you have or help you create some new ones. It is beautiful up here though, maybe you'll visit sometime?

I think you would find it very interesting; it's almost like a microclimate. The weather changes faster than I have time to think. It really is quite beautiful.

Yours sincerely,

Proff. Anderson

P.S. I'm sorry if I have already replied to this email; I seem to be losing time up here.

"He's inviting you out there. Are you actually considering this?"

The frustration in his voice was obvious. Sometimes I thought he really cared about me… more than just a friend. Was this just concern over my safety, or something else? It probably didn't help that he had also left the address of the cabin at the bottom of the email. Me and Anderson had become close after having a lot of similar scientific interests. We used to spend hours after class, batting ideas and opinions off each other. It was still professional, there was still a line, but it was a friendship, of sorts. Anderson had emailed me after the funeral telling me he was going up to spend some time in the cabin but would still be contactable if I needed help for my work. He told me where the cabin was if I wanted to visit to go through things. It seemed professional, it seemed normal. Lucas was making this something it wasn't.

"Yes, but that's not why I asked you to read this email. Look at the end, 'losing track of time'?" I replied quickly, hoping to redirect him.

"Yeah, what about it?" He muttered.

He was clearly still annoyed, but at what exactly? That I wasn't sure about. I pushed on.

"I didn't get it either. But last night, when I got back to my dorm, I re-read some of his other emails to me. They're all a bit strange. I can't put my finger on it… but I feel like something isn't right. And now he's not answering me."

"And let me guess, the other emails said how time blurred into itself up at the cabin because it's just *soo* beautiful and peaceful and perfect?"

I took a deep breath in. His lack of interest and clear aggravation at the emails were getting on my last nerve. I snatched my laptop back.

"No. They said he had been struggling with headaches up there. He also said there were things he couldn't remember. I don't know what he meant by that, he put it down to high pressure and the change of pollen. But I'm not convinced."

He stared at me blankly. "And this means you have to go and see him?"

I sighed in frustration. "No! Obviously not."

I paused for a moment, considering whether there was any point in even trying to continue this conversation. I decided to try one last time.

"Listen. I understand this probably sounds like nothing but excuses or that I'm looking into it too much, but we spent a lot of time together last year working on my thesis and research collection. I got to know him. He wasn't like this. And since what happened in the summer..."

Lucas stifled a laugh that made a ball of rage burn inside my chest.

"Mils, you didn't know him. Not, like, personally," he shook his head at me, eyes still fixed to the ground. "What happened in the summer?"

I could feel my eyes burning with tears that threatened to escape.

"His wife died, Lucas! Have some compassion."

Lucas's expression softened almost instantly as the words left my mouth, like he had forgotten that it had happened, or at least put it out of his memory. He knew how grief felt more than anyone, so hopefully he could understand why I was so concerned now.

He nodded his head. He didn't answer, he didn't need to. We sat there in silence for the rest of the break. I zoned out, staring at my reflection in the pond. As it rippled, I noticed it changed every emotion on my face, as if everything that I was feeling inside my reflection was showing me. I fixated on the movement until Lucas finished his baguette and got up to walk to his next lecture.

"So what do you think happened to him? He's just disappeared into thin air?" Lucas said, waving his hands like a puff of smoke, as we continued to walk along the pathway back to the lecture halls.

I was getting pretty frustrated at this point. I couldn't really make sense of this myself, but I hoped at least he would try to understand, try to get why it mattered.

"No, not disappeared. But maybe he's in a dark place mentally, and sitting up there alone not answering anyone isn't healthy. I don't think he has much of a support system."

Lucas looked at me, puzzled. "How do you know that?"

Silence.

I felt my cheeks flush. I hadn't meant to tell him that part.

"Last night, I couldn't stop thinking about him. Again, *not in that way*," I had to reiterate. "Why wouldn't he answer me when he's all alone in some cabin? It just made little sense to me. So… I found his sister on Facebook."

Lucas stopped. We had just arrived outside the first lecture hall where his next class was scheduled. I was hoping he would just walk inside and forget I had said anything. But he just stood there, staring at me, waiting for an answer.

"I messaged her," I admitted. "I asked when she had last heard from him."

I exhaled. There it was. I sounded completely insane. But I had to know. My professor was out there in a cabin all alone, and not in a great mental state. We had become very close last year. I would say we were friends, not that I would admit that to Lucas. I needed to know if he was okay.

"Mils!" Lucas shouted, a little too loudly, so that a few nosy students having chats in their small groups had turned to look at us.

I glanced around, embarrassed that everyone was now looking at me. I took his hand and led him through the doorway.

"Listen," I whispered, not wanting any more students to hear that I was going outright insane. "His sister replied. She said that she hadn't seen him or heard from him since a week ago. Apparently, he had called her every day since the funeral, but now he's just stopped."

Lucas looked stunned. I imagined he regretted getting out of bed this morning now.

"So what?" he finally said. "You think he's in trouble? Hurt himself? Maybe he just needed some space."

I felt drained. Surely, he must have understood how worried I was. He must have understood why I would want to know what's happened.

"Why would he message you and not his sister?" Lucas interrupted my thoughts.

"I don't know. Maybe because he trusts me? Maybe because I'm closer than she is? But don't you think this is all a bit worrying?"

Lucas threw his arms in the air with a look of pure disbelief on his face. "Closer? So, you two are like best friends now? And yes! I think it's worrying. But you can't do anything about it. Call the police to check in on him or something."

"No, closer in distance, Lucas!" I snapped.

The large, old clock at the end of the hall chimed one o'clock.

Lucas looked at the clock and then back at me. "I have to go. I can't be late for another class. We can talk about this later. I'm out of lectures at five. Meet me at my dorm after then."

He turned and walked along the large, dimly lit corridor towards the entrance of his lecture hall.

I watched him as he walked away. My head was spinning. I felt exhausted after trying to explain my feelings to him. I was worried and I had a gut feeling. That's all I knew. I just wanted him to support me.

I felt disheartened. I couldn't understand what his problem was. Wasn't he at all curious? I want to work this out together. I know something isn't right here. In that moment, I decided that with or without his support, I was going to find Anderson.

Chapter 3

Lucas

I was unsure whether my professor had said a word all class. All I could think about was Amelia. Her, and my weird dream last night. I was in the middle of a forest on my own, staring into a moonlit lake. It was so peaceful and beautiful, until the lake rippled. Until five long, thin fingers slowly emerged from the water. Frozen in fear, I couldn't move until the fingers shot out at me, grabbing me around the neck and dragging me into the lake. I woke up panting, feeling as if I was suffocating.

I shook my mind from my dream, trying to focus on something else. Anything else. Was she really going to go to that cabin to see Anderson during the autumn break? Wasn't that a bit...*strange?* I understood why, they shared an academic passion. And she was worried about him. But a professor and student alone in a remote cabin... that had to violate some sort of teaching code, *right?*

I couldn't let her go up there alone. What if something happened to her?

She was all I had left since my mum passed.

I rolled my eyes at myself and dropped my head into my hands. Nothing was going to happen to her. Because nothing *had* happened. Anderson hadn't disappeared. He had probably just switched his communications off. He probably just wanted some time alone. Everyone does. I understood that feeling, life can be overwhelming.

What's the worst that's going to happen? She'd spend a week away with her professor.

Share laughs.

Food, and...*a bed?*

I groaned as I started packing my bag to get to my next class. I couldn't think like that. She wouldn't do that. It was a purely professional relationship. Besides, he was at least two decades older than her.

I knew deep down I needed to trust her. I had no right to tell her what to do. But I wanted to keep her safe, and I wanted to avoid her getting hurt.

I zipped up my bag and headed towards my last lecture of the day. I promised myself that I would actually focus this time. That I'd stop letting my imagination spiral. I'd talk everything through with her later, properly. And it would all be fine.

I was sure it would all be fine.

I shook off my sodden hair as I walked through the door of my dorm. It had been pouring, and today I hadn't been as well prepared as

I had been last night. I set my bag down next to the umbrella that I *should* have picked up this morning, walked over to the mini-fridge, and grabbed a drink. I kicked the old fridge as I shut the door, stopping the knocking sound of its old gas pipes. Slumping into my cheap blue armchair, I let out a deep breath.

She would be here soon. We would talk. I'd tell her she needed to forget about the fact that he could be in trouble, he was probably fine.

We would talk about the cabin. She'd realise it was a terrible idea. Then she'd decide to spend the break here with me instead.

I smiled at my own delusion, knowing full well she was strong-headed and stubborn. She would argue her case and march off into the sunset with Anderson. This thought wiped the smile off my face pretty quickly.

A knock at the door snapped me out of it. I set my drink down, stood up, and plastered a big "I'm sorry" grin across my face before opening it.

She stood there, soaking wet. Her long hair clung flat to her cheeks, and mascara ran down her pink, flushed face. She was shivering so hard that she looked almost cartoonish.

She returned my smile, dropped her bag to the floor, and walked forward, straight into my arms.

I froze for a moment, then wrapped my arms around her. She was ice-cold and completely drenched. As she relaxed in my arms, I slowly walked backward, closing the door behind us.

I dropped back into my small armchair, and she fell with me, landing in my lap.

We both started laughing like we both used to, like we always did.

She pushed herself up and perched on my leg, wiping the soggy strands of hair away from her face. She looked up at me and I looked back, heart hammering. I could stay here forever. In her arms. In her laughter. And, more importantly, she was *here*. Not with Anderson. Not at the cabin. With me.

I loved her. Not just physically, though, of course, she was beautiful. The way she smiled, slightly asymmetrically. The constellation of freckles scattered across her cheeks. Light and barely visible, but there all the same. The way her face would light up. The way her eyes would sparkle when she talked about something she loved, especially when she was talking to me. But it wasn't just her face. I loved her mind. The way she questioned everything. The way she needed to understand everything. The way she wouldn't let things lie, not when the truth might still be out there.

I knew then, as I watched her, that she would not let this go. Not Anderson. Not the emails, or lack thereof. Not the cabin.

And I would be there to support her. All the way.

"I'm sorry," she said, looking away from me, clearly embarrassed, snapping me out of my thoughts.

"No, you have nothing to be sorry for. I'm sorry for how I reacted. It was just… a lot to take in, you know?" I said, brushing a strand of wet hair from her cheek. "I want to talk about this. I want to know more about your relationship and about Anderson, you two are clearly close."

She blushed and looked at the floor before hopping off my lap and pulling my desk chair in front of me.

Did she know how I felt about her?

Sometimes I thought she did. Other times, I was convinced she did not know. And I couldn't risk ruining what we had by telling her.

I cleared my throat and took a sip of my drink. It was already going warm.

"So, tell me more!" I said in my usual overdramatic, gossipy tone that always made her laugh.

"Okay, so, you know he was helping me with my dissertation and research," she said, pausing, waiting for me to answer.

"Yes, I know about that, and the fact you two spent a lot of time together," I continued with mock seriousness.

She smiled. "You know about the email Anderson sent back to me... and that he invited me to his cabin. *For help with my research.*"

"Yesss..." I tried to stay in character, but the way she said 'for research' hit me like a punch in the stomach.

"And you remember I said there was something that felt... off? About the emails?" she continued.

"You mean there's *more* to it that feels off than him losing track of time and forgetting things?" I asked. "Is that even possible?"

If it were and there were more to the emails, why had she waited until now to voice her concerns?

Amelia hesitated.

"Read this one he sent me the other day," she said at last.

She pulled her laptop out of her bag, scrolled, typed, and passed it over to me.

The dorm room lights flickered slightly, just as my heart palpitated. I began to read the email.

Dear Amelia,

I have to say, being out here isn't as difficult as I thought it would be. I'm not all alone; I have my Lucy, and the tulips. So don't you worry about me!

Yes, to answer your question, the weathers very erratic up here, it's very interesting. I think you would love it, something's very special about this place. I'm unsure whether I want to come home!

Anyway, speak soon! Send me over that paper you found, and I'll have a look to see if it'll be suitable.

Yours sincerely,

Prof. Anderson

P.S. I was looking into the lake, and I believe I noticed something strange. It was probably just my imagination, though. But I am sure I saw something. Maybe it was just my reflection. But I can't stop thinking about it. Sometimes out here, I feel like I'm being watched.

Anyway, I thought I would just share in case anything comes of it.

I sat back, trying to keep a neutral expression. Trying to wrap my head around what I'd just read. My mind reeled with emotions. I couldn't choose which one to settle on.

"So," Amelia asked. "What do you think?"

I wanted to say Anderson sounded crazy. He needed help. I wanted to say that I was angry that he was putting this all on her, that he was trying to weirdly persuade her to go and see him. But I couldn't say any of that.

"Why, now, do you think this email is weird? Why didn't you think anything of it last week when he sent it? Because yes, it is…strange. Who's Lucy?" I asked.

It was all I could think of saying. Amelia looked visibly annoyed. "Because he has always been slightly odd. He's a character to say the least. I thought he was just being a bit eccentric, not losing the plot!" She stood and began pacing the room. "Lucy was his wife," she continued. "I thought maybe he meant she was with me in spirit, or in his thoughts. But the more I read this email, I'm not sure."

"Yeah, I mean, it is worrying. I know what it feels like to lose someone. To isolate yourself and feel like you're completely alone," I said, beginning to change my mind about Anderson.

The more I read, the slightly more worried I became. Amelia nodded slowly and perched on the arm of the sofa, her gaze fixed on the ground, her expression unreadable.

We sat there for a moment. Yes, this was weird. But if I put my selfish jealousy aside, was this man actually trying to reach out for help? Maybe he wasn't doing okay up there on his own.

Sometimes, out here, I feel like I'm being watched.

I couldn't shake this sentence from my head.

"I'm a bit concerned about his mental state, being up there in that cabin alone…it can't be good." I finally admitted.

My cheeks burned red. I didn't like admitting I was wrong, but it was better to do that than have a man suffer out there alone.

She let out a sigh of relief. Was it because I was finally supporting her, or because I wasn't talking about her going to the cabin anymore? I wasn't sure, but she looked calmer now.

"What do you think I should do?" She asked, twirling a lock of hair between her fingers.

I paused, considering. I could convince her to report her concerns to the head of the department. Cease contact. Or I could drop the jealousy and think like a human being, about someone possibly losing their mind in isolation. I decided to choose the latter.

"I think you should email him again. Ask how he's doing. Ask him to describe exactly what he believes to have seen out there," I said, reaching out and placing a hand on her knee. "Then we will know how to deal with this situation and how to best help him… if he answers."

She stopped playing with her hair and leaned into me, resting her head on my shoulders.

I put a hand on her head and started playing with her hair. Maybe protecting her didn't mean holding her back, but walking beside her, even when it scared me.

"And then," I continued, "I think we should order a large pizza, some wings… and start a *Saw* movie marathon."

I loved our horror movie nights together. We would eat an array of fried and unhealthy foods, gossip and laugh, and share memories. Become closer. Amelia smiled and wrapped her arms around my neck.

"And garlic bread," she whispered into my ear.

I laughed as she leapt off the chair to grab a takeaway menu.

Chapter 4

Amelia

I wasn't really a big fan of horror movies, but I learned to love the comfort they brought Lucas. I had just gotten back to my dorm after falling asleep at Lucas's during the third *Saw* movie.

After his mum passed, our weekly horror marathons became his escape, and my way of being there for him. He needed a support system after the trauma. I was the first person he had called.

I could still hear his voice from that night; broken, shaking, barely getting the words out. The way his voice cracked mid-sentence. The way I could hear his breath catching through the speaker as he tried not to cry. He hadn't said much, he didn't need to. The silence said it all.

That call changed everything. In that moment, I promised myself I would do everything I could to support him, no matter what. I never wanted to hear him talk like that again. I never wanted to see him fall apart like that again, like the moment he first laid his eyes on me when

I turned up at the hospital for him. The sterile, clinical smell stung my nose as I walked through the door in the hospital to see him standing there, beside her body. The second he saw me, he collapsed. He didn't say a word. He clutched my coat as he fell to his knees, destroyed. Unable to let go of me for what felt like an eternity, as if he were clutching onto his last real thing in his world. Like I was the only thing left tethering him to reality.

I would do anything to protect him. That was just over a year ago now, and I have watched him go through all the emotions. Even months after it happened, long after the funeral, I would still glimpse the pain he tried so hard to hide. The moments he would turn away mid-conversation, shoulders tensing and blinking hard. Or those rare times I noticed a tear escaping down his cheek when he thought I wasn't looking.

He didn't like talking about it. And to be honest, I didn't either. He barely even said her name anymore. But I remembered everything as if it were yesterday.

I wiped the tears from my cheeks that had escaped from the memories. After putting my laptop on charge, I got dressed. I was relieved that Lucas was finally out of his mood, finally supportive of my decisions. I was still unsure of what I was going to do, or how I was going to handle any of this. But with his support, I knew I would make the right decision, whatever that looked like.

Unlocking the door of my dorm, I drew in a deep breath. The small dorm room was my solitude, and as much as I loved spending time with Lucas, I loved my own time too. I threw on my oversized jumper and fluffy socks, curling up in the large armchair in the back

44

corner of my room. While I waited for my laptop to charge, I leant over and cracked open the window. The rain had settled during the night, and the crisp after-storm chill still lingered in the air. The sky was clear, and the morning sun peeked over the buildings opposite the window. I watched as the birds flew from tree to tree, exchanging their usual morning greetings. The campus was deathly quiet now. That's how I liked it.

Most of the students had gone home this weekend, ready for the autumn break. I knew Lucas would stay here, he had no home to return to anymore, not really. So, usually, I stayed too. I enjoyed the quiet anyway.

A rustling at the end of my bed pulled my attention away from the silent sunrise. I turned my head to check if Snowy was okay. He looked up at me with his big black eyes from inside his cage. His little pink nose twitched as he smelt around for the breakfast I had yet to give him. I cooed my good mornings to him as I shuffled around the room to fill his bowl with rabbit pellets and refresh his water. I placed the bowl inside his cage as his attention quickly shifted from me to his morning feast. Smiling, I ruffled his white fluff, which annoyed him, and he shook his head, ears flopping. I love this little rabbit. I brought him when I moved into my new room. Despite a few friends being around campus, I knew no one in my dorm. Having nightly cuddles with Snowy drowned out the loneliness that the evenings brought. Plus, it was easy to hide his cage under my bed when we had a dorm inspection.

I drew a slow, deep breath as my laptop lit up, humming back to life. Pulling myself up from watching Snowy chew his pellets, I walked back over to my chair by the window and began scrolling through my social media pages. They were now full of photos of the other students at home with their families across England, and across continents for some. I missed home, I missed my mum and dad.

Picking up my phone, I tapped out a text to Mum: "Miss you. Will call soon."

My mum, always understanding, had never pressured me to come home. Both my parents were doctors, familiar with the toll grief could take, even months later.

They were also very busy, so I doubted they would give much notice to another week of me not being there. They were so supportive of me when I had told them what had happened to Lucas. They gave me things to say, things to talk about, and advice on how to handle certain conversations in a way that wouldn't further upset him. I had never experienced the hurt of losing someone to suicide myself and hadn't met anyone that had done so before Lucas, although the rumours around Anderson's wife's death had been speculated to be as such.

I put my phone down, knowing my mum wouldn't answer me anytime soon, and focused back on my laptop.

Opening my emails, I scrolled past the usual junk; discount codes and online sales and paused when I saw two unread messages.

From Professor Anderson.

Two emails. Same day.

How had I missed these? They were dated two days ago.

I frowned. That was odd. I hovered over the emails. Why two? A small part of me hoped it was him saying he was coming home, that it was all some kind of joke or elaborate prank. But deep down, I knew better.

A pit formed in my stomach. Was he okay?

I guessed he didn't really have many people checking in on him. He mentioned no friends or family other than his wife, Lucy, and his sister, Charlotte, and I knew he hadn't spoken to her. But then again, would a professor really mention that to his student?

I was unsure.

Our past interactions came to mind. I had known him, professionally, for about two and a half years now. At first glance, it all seemed pretty normal. He was just Professor Anderson; a little intense, always buried in his work, always diverted between conversations, and occasionally oblivious to social cues, but brilliant all the same. He was always scrawling down notes and ideas in his journal; he would even stop mid-conversation to do so.

He was just Professor Anderson.

But now, as I was sifting through my memories, I wasn't completely sure. Was he always a bit... off, or was he just an eccentric genius?

I recalled the way he would sometimes lose track of conversations mid-sentence, his mind always two conversations ahead of the one he was having. Full of overly long pauses in his replies.

At the time, I just thought that they were his personality quirks. But now...

Still, my fingers hovered over the first subject line. I clicked and read. My heart sank. My chest tightened, nausea rising with every sentence. I'd always had an overactive imagination, but this felt different. This wasn't just paranoia. This was real. He wasn't okay. Lucas had been right; being alone out there for that long wasn't healthy. Anderson needed help. He needed someone to speak to. Someone trained. Someone professional. Was it hallucinations? Delusions? Maybe worse. My skin ran cold as I re-read the emails. He would repeat himself. He sounded erratic, as if he wanted me to know what he was thinking but was also trying to hide it at the same time. I wanted to go there and help him. I needed to.

Closing my laptop, I continued to stare out the window, searching for an answer in the morning sky. Searching for a solution I knew wouldn't be there. I unfocused my gaze and looked at my reflection in the window. My reflection stared back. The familiar oval face. My scruffy hair that was thrown into a bun on my head. The slightly flushed cheeks. My deep caramel eyes.

I know this girl. The girl who would always put other people first. I would help him. I had to.

I had tried calling Lucas, but guessed he was still asleep. I decided to grab us both a coffee before heading back over to his. I blew a few kisses to Snowy before grabbing my bag and heading out. As I walked towards the campus cafe, worries twisted in my chest like tangled vines. The cafe was nearly empty, with just a lone student writing on their laptop in the corner. What I would give for my only worries to be writing an assignment right now. The scent of coffee grounds mixed with vanilla syrup danced around me, so normal it now felt so strange. How could everything still be so normal?

I headed to the counter, clearing my throat to grab the attention of the barista, who was more focused on her phone than her surroundings. I ordered my drinks and sat at a nearby table.

As I waited for our coffees, I noticed the eerie silence in the room. Only the coffee machine and a faint buzz of electricity hummed from the lights above. The sounds all began to fade as I drifted off into my own mind.

I was raised to care about people. To help others before myself. Raised in a family of doctors, I had seen the depths of love and care people could have for others — and the cost of it.

I heard my parents talk about death, terminal diagnoses, and the cold, clinical way they had to deliver devastating news to families. I'd watched the weight it put on them, saw how love and care could both heal and break a person. I watched my mum cry in the kitchen after work, on hold to a family that had called her in their grief for answers. She muffled her cries and steadied herself before putting on a clinical tone to retake the phone call. A kind act, a heartbreaking one, but kind all the same.

I always wondered, did I want that life too?

I decided I didn't, I still wanted to help people, the environment, animals. Anything really, I just wanted to help. That's why I chose this course. But I couldn't do what my parents did. I wasn't strong enough.

I was unable to watch someone going through pain and not be there to support them, even if it weighed on me.

The barista called my name, snapping me out of my thoughts. I smiled faintly and thanked them.

Two large cappuccinos in hand, I headed out the door, towards Lucas's building.

I rehearsed my thoughts carefully. Anything that involved someone's mental health had to be handled delicately with Lucas. And this, this was delicate.

I wondered if it would be safe to go down there if Anderson wasn't of sound mind. Should I call the authorities instead, or another professor, perhaps?

I didn't know. I only knew that I couldn't ignore it. I needed to help him in one way or another.

Was I really equipped to handle something like this? I hoped I wouldn't make it worse.

When I reached Lucas's door, I hesitated. My hand hovered over the buzzer, then fell away. I stepped back.

I imagined Lucas's reaction to the emails; angry, or worse, crumbling to his knees in grief as the emotions brought back memories of his mum. What if he laughed it off? Or maybe he would shut down, like he used to when anyone brought up his mum. He used to be so adventurous before she passed. He would be jumping at the chance to investigate something obscure and outrageous like this. But now, I just didn't know. He had planned a hike up Snowdon before she passed. One day, he wanted to complete the three peaks challenge. He'd cancelled the trip. At this rate, I didn't think he would ever re-plan it again.

Instead of going in, I sat on the bench outside his building, letting the cold seep into my legs. I needed a minute. Maybe two. I didn't want to speak yet. I didn't want to influence him.

Anderson's words were calm, too calm. Like someone trying to convince himself more than anyone else.

Lucas and I would read the emails together.

Then we'd decide what to do.

As I sat there, the light wind around me steadied. The birds stopped their beautiful tweeting. There was no movement in the air, no noise. Like the world had stopped turning. An eerie sense of dread washed through my body.

Chapter 5

Lucas

I woke up to a knock on the door. Disoriented, I rolled over to look at the empty bed behind me. I had taken the sofa, which offered no mercy to my back. I figured Amelia must have woken up early to grab some coffee. Stretching my body, I sat up and blinked my sleepy haze away.

I padded to the door and opened it. Sure enough, there she was, holding two large takeaway coffee cups. I smiled and moved to the side, letting her through the door.

The smell of the dark-roasted beans hit my nostrils — rich, earthy, and just a little burnt. Even the scent alone was enough to wake me up properly. It wrapped around the room like a familiar blanket, but it couldn't warm the chill that clung to the windows. Outside, the light was thin and grey. The kind of light that didn't quite banish the shadows. It was a chilly morning, and the radiator clicked but never warmed fully. Damp clung to the windows like fingerprints, fogged and unrelenting. I shivered, wrapping my arms around myself.

Amelia's jumper was damp at the edges, her cheeks wind-kissed and flushed. But her eyes, they were distant. Alert. Like someone who'd heard something they shouldn't have.

She set the drinks down on the desk and turned to face me. A strange expression washed over her face, a look that made something in my stomach twinge. The look wasn't an unfamiliar one, but not a common one either. I hadn't seen this one since the day she turned up to see me at the hospital after my mum passed. Something was off. The look someone gives when they're about to break news that might not have a fix.

"Are you okay?" I asked, sitting down beside her on the desk chair, wrapping my hands around the warm cup.

"Yeah, I'm—I think so," she answered, twirling a loose strand of hair around her fingers.

I reached over and gently stilled her hand. "Tell me what's wrong."

She pulled her hand away, hesitant, and reached for her bag. Her laptop came out. She opened it, scrolled, and then turned it towards me. She hesitated, her fingers fidgeting on the keyboard. "Please… just read this."

I frowned, pulling the laptop closer to me. She hadn't had issues telling me what was on her mind before. Why was she being so cryptic now? So cautious?

As my eyes scanned the email, I got my answer.

Dear Amelia,

I need your help, or someone's help. I'm not sure. I can't begin to explain the strange things that are happening out here. I went to the lake. I hoped to see her again, but she wasn't there this time. I saw something else. I can't explain this well.

I saw my reflection in the lake, but it wasn't my reflection. It was too real. Not opaque like a reflection, not shimmering like water, like I was really standing in front of me. But this was not me, not really. It looked the same as me, but the smile… it had this twisted, big smile and its eyes, its eyes were hollow. Lifeless. Dead.

I don't think I can sleep anymore, not at night anyway. I'm going to try and keep the curtains shut from now on, I don't want my reflection to see me.

I can't explain this well. It felt so… sinister. Sometimes I don't even feel alone anymore.

If you come here, I can explain in more detail. Maybe I can show you.

Yours sincerely,

Prof. Anderson

I sat and stared at the screen in silence. Words crawled into my brain and sat there, heavy and impossible to move. I remembered the hours spent trying to make sense of my mother's messages. She had insisted that the TV spoke to her. She locked doors. The quiet sobbing that she could hear through the walls.

And now here I was again, staring down a screen, reading sentences that felt like déjà vu.

Was this a cry for help, or something worse? Something… real?

I wanted to dismiss it, to chalk it up to stress, overwork, a mind fraying at the edges. But my mother had started the same way. One strange comment, one sleepless night, one shadow she swore was a man. It had spiralled so quickly.

"I'm sorry I had to show you this," Amelia said, her voice quiet, as if she could feel the storm brewing inside me.

I didn't reply. Not yet. She scrolled down to the next email and turned the laptop to face me again.

Dear Amelia,

Thank you for, hopefully, understanding my last email. I feel you won't judge me for the things I have experienced out here, and I trust you'll stay open-minded. I do ask of you not to share my overactive imagination with the other professors at the university. I fear I will be laughed out of my career or seen as a madman.

I haven't slept. I don't think I've even blinked. My reflection didn't blink. I check the windows every hour. Sometimes I think I'm the reflection and it's the real me is the one watching. Please don't tell anyone. They'll come for me. There have been… strange happenings out here, I will admit, and I will share with you when you arrive.

I know how this must sound. Again, I think I would like to put this down to my imagination, but it will surely give you a laugh at your old crazy professor anyhow.

Yours sincerely,

Prof. Anderson

We sat there in silence. The weight of those words hung in the air between us, pressing against our chests like smoke. I subconsciously tapped my fingers on the side of the sofa, like a ticking time bomb. Amelia twirled her hair around her fingers, faster and faster in motion. I thought back to my first year. Anderson had stayed late one night to help me fix a poorly written assignment, two hours before the submission deadline. "Brilliance needs patience," he'd said, handing me a USB with a soft smile. I hadn't forgotten that. Five minutes passed, though it felt like an hour, before I finally spoke.

"He needs help."

Amelia nodded slowly. "Yeah, I think so too," she said, exhaling. "How do we help him though? Shall we… call someone?"

"No," I said immediately, shaking my head. "I've seen what happens when people are in this kind of state. They get labelled, medicated, locked away. I've seen it. My mum…" I trailed off, the thought too raw to say out loud.

"If he's alone out there and really losing his grip-" Amelia began.

"Then we need to get to him first. Before anyone else does," I finished. "We need to assess the situation ourselves. Bring him home if we can."

Amelia perched on my lap and wrapped her arms around my neck, pressing her face into my shoulder. "I agree," she whispered. "I'm just scared. You know, it's freaking me out. I want to help him, but also, is this too big for us? What if we can't help him?"

I sat staring at my hands in my lap, my mind twisting with possibilities and outcomes. Amelia sighed. "How are we going to get there?"

"I'll drive," I said. "I'm not losing another person to their own mind."

I didn't say her name. I didn't have to. Amelia's hand tightened on my arm, her silence saying more than any words could.

I remembered the doctor's voice after my mum's final breakdown, detached and professional. "She'll be safer here," they'd said. But safer didn't mean healed.

What if Anderson didn't need a padded room? What if he needed someone to believe him, even just a little bit?

We agreed to meet at my car after we had both packed. I couldn't shake the nervous feeling that I had bitten off more than I could chew. What if she was right and they couldn't help him? If he had really spiralled, I didn't know if we would truly be safe. I couldn't find the answers in my own head, but deep down I knew the right thing to do. I needed to go; I could just feel it.

I hoped to make it in one go. I stuffed energy drinks into my rucksack like my life depended on them, because maybe it did. Alongside them went a toothbrush, some clean clothes, my phone charger, and a half-used bottle of body wash. It wasn't much, but it didn't need to be.

I zipped up my bag, my hands moving faster than my thoughts. A tightness had settled into my chest, a pressure that didn't ease even when I checked and double-checked the contents.

My fingers hovered over a small utility knife on the edge of the drawer. I stared at it, hesitated.

Don't be ridiculous.

But my hand closed over it, anyway. I shook the thought away and tucked the knife into my desk drawer.

My eyes landed on the small, framed photo on my desk, the one of me with my mum. The photo was taken the day I was accepted into the university. She'd asked the waiter at the restaurant to take the photo during dinner. She looked so proud. So alive. It was only a few weeks before the sickness started.

I picked it up, holding it in both hands. One corner of the frame had chipped, and a year of handling had smudged the glass. My thumb ran over her face, a moment frozen in time. Her eyes sparkled with pride. I remembered the exact laugh she'd given after that photo, the half-snort kind that she used to do when truly happy. The laugh had disappeared long before she did.

"Would you still be here if I hadn't left?" I whispered, my voice barely audible.

I could still hear her voice on those voicemails, insisting the neighbours were watching her. The sharp click of the locks. The rustle of curtains being tugged shut over and over. I'd lived that cycle once before. Could I do it again?

Mental illness had stolen her away from me slowly, like fog creeping in under the door until it swallowed the room whole. I wouldn't let it do that to someone else I knew again. Not to Anderson. Not if I could help it.

I grabbed my jacket and threw it on. Carefully, I tucked the photo into my bag, slung it over my shoulder, grabbed my keys, and left.

I stared at the doorway before leaving, heart hammering. I'd left too late once before. Too slow, too unsure. The nurses had told me she'd been asking for me in her last moments. I couldn't let someone else down.

I walked out the door and took a deep breath as it locked behind me. Fresh air filled my lungs and cleared the fog in my mind. A small rustling sound to my left snapped me back to reality as I turned to see where it was coming from. A small robin sitting in the thick bush's branches, its wings twitched and head turned to the side as if it were studying me. My lips curled into a soft smile and a warmness filled my chest, extinguishing the anxiety that sat there before it.

"I'll help him, Mum, don't worry."

My eyes lingered on the bird for a few seconds longer before I finally took off to start our rescue mission.

This trip would not be easy. But I knew one thing: Amelia would be beside me. And that made it easier.

Chapter 6

Amelia

As I zipped my bag, a heaviness settled in my chest. What if we're too late? The thought came uninvited and lodged itself firmly in my mind. He might be injured or have hurt himself. He could have fled the cabin in search for help.

I shoved a jumper into my backpack too roughly and had to repack it. My hands wouldn't stop shaking. What if this is one of those things you read about after the fact "If only someone had checked in sooner…" I shook off the thought. I had to meet Lucas by the car, so I couldn't fall apart yet.

I checked my phone to see if Charlie had replied. When doing my course introduction, she was the first friend I met. Given her persistent belief that Lucas and I would pair well, I figured our impending 'trip' would excite her and hoped she would jump at the chance to look after my rabbit. She also loved Snowy and never turned down a chance for soft bunny cuddles. I also couldn't imagine my fluff-ball would be too happy being stuck in his cage the entire drive to the cabin. My phone pinged as I stared at it, the screen lighting up with her name. After a lot of 'Oh my god's!' and 'How cute's' she had agreed I could drop off Snowy for a little sleep over at her dorm. I didn't tell her the true reason we were going on this trip, not completely anyway. I figured some things were better kept between myself and Lucas for now.

I packed Snowy's food and toys into a bag whilst he sat there side-eyeing me, like he knew. I threw my backpack over my shoulder, putting Snowy's bag on top of his cage as I struggled to lift it and close the door behind me. Luckily, Charlie lived 2 dorms over, so carrying the furry lump was short-lived. She greeted me at the door with a smile as I walked through the doorway and placed his cage down on her desk.

"Are you looking forward to your little romantic getaway then?" Charlie teased with a sparkle in her eye.

Rolling my eyes, I opened Snowy's cage to give him a kiss goodbye.

"You know it's not a romantic trip. You know we're just friends," I grumbled, face full of the white fur on top of my bunny's head. Charlie's smile never faltered.

"Of course. I know. The cosy cabin with a hand-built fire. Snuggled under a blanket with a hot chocolate whilst the rain trickles down the windows. Long walks through the chilly forest. I'm sureee you'll come back as just friends," her tone tipped from teasing to sarcastic, her hand gestures big and dramatic.

She always thought me and Lucas would be cute together. I know she's loving this even more than she's letting on. I chose not to feed into her fantasy and gave her a big hug.

"Thank you for this. I'll text you when I get there," I said, making my way swiftly out the door before she could swoon over the misinterpretation of mine and Lucas's trip any longer.

"See you soon! Mrs *Hunter,*" she called to me from the doorway, and I hurried out of the hallway.

I smiled to myself as I made my way to Lucas's car. Admittedly, I had thought about me and Lucas being more than friends, but it just was never the right moment. He needed a friend more than ever.

After waiting by the car for a few minutes, I threw on my jumper, hoping he wouldn't be too much longer. The weather had turned again. That's the great thing about English weather: it could be a beautiful morning one minute and chucking it down without so much as a warning the next.

By the time Lucas had reached the car, the heavens had opened like a fire sprinkler. Rain lashed the windscreen in rhythmic bursts, like a thousand ticking clock's I couldn't see.

I slid into the passenger seat, rain soaking my jeans instantly before I could get the door shut. The wet coldness suffocated my thighs, heavy and tight, just like the doubt that had pooled in my chest.

He tossed our bags into the back and jumped into the driver's seat.

"Ready?" Lucas asked, glancing sideways at me, his voice steady but his eyes uncertain.

I hesitated for a moment, a knot tightening in my stomach. I thought I was ready. I knew I wanted to go, that I had to go. But was I biting off more than I could chew? Should I have told someone? A professional?

"Ready." I finally replied, the word small but final, hanging in the damp air between us.

The first few hours of the car journey were mostly just terrible traffic, stop-start chaos getting out of London and the surrounding areas. But once we had hit the M25, it was smooth sailing. I rested my head against the window, watching the rain dance along the glass, each droplet sliding into the next as if they were racing to the edge. The late-autumn countryside unfurled outside with golden-hued trees, drenched meadows, and sleepy fields veiled in grey mist.

I watched the horses grazing, their coats dark and soaked, huddling beneath the makeshift wooden shelters that dotted the landscape like relics of calm. In the distance, sheep stood still as stone, dotting the hills like cotton balls stuck to the earth. A sudden movement caught my eye. Two deer darting up the thicket, their elegant bodies barely a whisper against the trees.

One deer stopped and turned its head, holding its gaze longer than it should have. For a second, I swore it was watching me, not startled, just… aware.

I blinked. It was gone. But the moment clung to me like the mist.

I began to count the sheep as they passed.

One sheep, two sheep, three…

Before I realised it, my eyelids had grown heavy. My internal dialogue faded into a blur of green and grey.

I didn't know how long I'd been asleep when I jolted awake, the car swaying gently with the road. I looked over at Lucas, and my stomach twinged. He hadn't slept, just kept driving, wide-eyed and overstimulated. He took a swig from a dented Redbull can, then tossed it behind him with the others. The sound of metal clinking on metal suggested that it wasn't his first.

"Did you want me to take over?" My voice came out sleepier than I had intended, which can't have helped him given his circumstances.

Lucas snorted and looked over at me. "I would… if you had a licence"

"Yeah, well, I still know how to drive," I retorted, flashing him a sleepy smile.

"Yeah, well, I would like to survive this trip," he countered, nudging me lightly.

I rolled my eyes at him and then turned to look out the window. Streetlights had started to flicker on. The sky was sinking into night.

A crow exploded from the hedgerow just as we passed, soaring so close to the windscreen that I winced before it disappeared into the mist.

Lucas flinched as he tried to steady the steering wheel, braking to slow his speed. My heart jumped.

"Well, that's a good omen," I muttered, trying to laugh. I couldn't.

"How much longer do we have?" I asked, biting my lip.

I was beginning to feel nervous. The idea of navigating a forest at night, after everything we'd read and seen, made my stomach twist.

"About 4 more hours, m'lady," Lucas said in his best chauffeur impression, tipping an invisible hat.

"Ohhh, that's a long time," I pulled the hood of my jumper further around my ears for false security.

Lucas nodded. "Yes. Yes, it is."

Outside, the trees blurred past. The road seemed to stretch on forever.

"And it's going to be dark pretty soon," I added, beginning to chew on my nail.

Lucas side-eyed me.

"Yes, yes it is," he repeated the words slowly, his tone flat with mock seriousness.

"Do you think we could stop off at one of the hotels at the next rest stop?" I asked. "You need to rest... and I'm two sips of water away from a disaster."

Lucas smirked. "There it is."

I kicked off my shoes as I raced into the hotel room to secure the best bed, which, frankly, was a low bar. Two single beds, a brown floral curtain, and a bedside lamp that buzzed like a trapped fly. Still, the one closest to the plug socket would be mine.

I threw my laptop on charge and flopped onto the mattress with a soft groan.

Outside, the storm had finally passed. Only the distant sounds of lorries humming along the motorway and a couple arguing in the car park disturbed the still night.

"Do you think this place has Wi-Fi?" I asked, eyeing the blinking router box as if it might just tell me the answer.

Lucas, who had just headed straight for the bathroom, shouted back, "I'm not sure this place even has a working bathroom light." Flicking all the switches on the bathroom wall.

Something about the quiet felt wrong. I snorted and pulled out my phone, trying to tether my laptop to its hotspot. Lucas returned and collapsed onto the second-best bed in the room with a sigh.

"I thought you had to pee?" he asked.

Instantly a gasp left me, the painful fullness of my bladder taking over my thoughts. "Oh my God, I still do!"

I leapt up and darted to the bathroom, flicking the light switch on my first try. Lucas tore into the crisps with loud crinkles, the only genuine sound in the room.

"What did you say to Anderson in the end?"

"I… didn't. I forgot," I called from the bathroom.

He paused mid-chew. The silence that followed hummed louder than the heater. I ran across the room and opened my inbox. Just as I was about to type, a new email blinked into view.

From Anderson.

No subject. No preview text. Just the name.

I froze, unable to figure out my next move. Something in my stomach shifted, a quiet twist, like the wrong note in a song.

"He's just emailed me," I murmured. My voice came out quieter than I had meant.

Lucas looked up. "What does it say?"

My fingers hovered above the trackpad, unwilling to move.

"Amelia?"

I clicked.

DON'T COME HERE.

That was it. No greeting. No signature. No sign-off.

Just those three words.

They stared back at me like a threat.

I stared at the screen, my skin crawling. I couldn't really understand what it meant. Of course, I knew what the words meant, obviously, but why? Why now?

"What did he say?" Lucas asked, sensing my shift in energy.

I slowly turned the screen towards him in silence.

"Don't come here," Lucas read out loud.

I blinked at him, completely baffled. "Yes, Lucas. I can read it. What does he mean?"

Lucas raised his hands defensively. "I was just making sure we were both reading the same thing!" he mocked.

"Probably means we shouldn't go," Lucas muttered, but didn't look up from the email. His fingers tapped the side of the bed like a metronome. I let out a sigh. He wasn't wrong, but he was frustrating.

"I think this means we need to go now more than ever, Mils," Lucas said gently. "Before things spiral further. He needs us."

I nodded, but my throat was tight. "I agree. But… this is scaring me."

We both lay in silence for a long while after that, the hum of the heater filling the quiet. Tomorrow would not be an easy day.

Our simultaneous alarms woke us both with a shock. I hadn't even realised I'd drifted off. It must have happened somewhere between worrying and watching the clock inch further towards morning, I imagined.

I got out of bed and stumbled towards the bathroom, jumped in the shower, and got dressed quickly. As I went to pack my bag, I shook Lucas awake, who had clearly fallen back asleep after snoozing his alarm. He groaned from under the covers, reaching blindly for an energy drink on the bedside table. He slowly got out of bed and headed towards the bathroom. I heard the sudden rush of water as the shower turned on. I sat on the edge of the bed, staring at the blank TV screen. What if Anderson wasn't even there anymore?

What if we opened the cabin door and found nothing? Or worse, signs he'd been there, and left. Or was taken...

Guilt started creeping in like a slow fog, mixing with the fear and nausea that sat in my stomach.

I should've emailed sooner. I should've called him when the first message came through.

I ran my hands through my hair, heart thudding harder with every possibility my mind conjured. What if I dragged Lucas into something we couldn't walk away from? I glanced toward the bathroom, where the shower still ran. I had a few more minutes. Just enough time to spiral.

By the time we had packed up and started the car, my thoughts were racing. I couldn't remember a time I had ever been this anxious.

My overactive imagination was in full swing as we passed more meadows and horses.

I wondered whether we would be greeted with open arms and thanks for our journey up to rescue him from his own mind. Or whether we would be greeted with something much more sinister. The *'Here's Johnny'* scene, from the time Lucas made me watch *The Shining*, flashed to my mind. I reminded myself that I needed to get him into a more comforting genre of movie.

I glanced over at Lucas. He was chewing his thumbnail, tapping the wheel.

"If you keep twirling your hair like that, you'll have none left," he muttered.

I instantly un-twirled my hair from my fingers. "Sorry. I'm just... a bit anxious"

"Yeah. Me too". He admitted. "We only have about an hour and a half to go"

Great, just enough time to dream up a hundred more ways this could go wrong. I leaned my head against the glass, slumping further into my chair. My phone flickered. Not the screen, but the flashlight, blinking once without being touched.

"Did you see that?" I asked Lucas as I checked my phone.

"See what?" he asked, as he kept his eyes fixed on the road ahead.

"Nothing, I guess," I dropped my phone back into my lap as I sunk back into my chair.

I watched the animals in the fields as they passed us. For a moment, one of the sheep looked wrong. Its head tilted back too far, neck bent at an impossible angle… and then it turned, looking perfectly normal again. Had it really turned, or had it just wanted me to think so?

"Sleep deprivation," I whispered to myself. But my stomach remained tight. I let my view of the sheep in the passing fields count me down to an uneasy sleep.

Chapter 7

Lucas

As the tarmac turned to gravel, I drove slightly uphill towards the blinking blue dot on my map. The trees thickened, and I climbed higher. Overgrown and wild, the road narrowed. The treeline closed in around us like a slow exhale from nature itself. I was already deep in the middle of nowhere. Fifteen more minutes, my phone said. The surrounding forest echoed with the occasional birdcall, broken only by the soft rumble of the engine and the crunch of gravel under my tyres. I couldn't help but imagine living somewhere like this. Quiet. Off the beaten track. No traffic, no emails, no grey concrete stretching to the horizon. Just me and Amelia.

The wheels buckled slightly beneath us as I rolled over a patch of thick, sticky mud. I felt my tyres sink a little, but I kept going. I hadn't renewed my roadside recovery, a gamble on my part. Not that I minded the risk. I just didn't want to look like an idiot in front of Amelia.

Two rabbits darted onto the road, chasing each other like children let loose. My foot slammed on the brakes. The car jolted, the engine choking into silence. Amelia stirred in the passenger seat, groggy. I turned the key; nothing happened. Again. Silence.

My heart thudded louder than the rain tapping on the windshield yesterday. Had I jinxed a breakdown?

With one more turn of the key and the engine coughed back to life. Relief calmed my stiff body, quickly tainted by unease.

A sickening dread came over me and settled in my gut like an unwelcome passenger. I don't know why. The feeling made no sense. This place is peaceful. A sunlit forest and harmless animals in the middle of the day. What was there to be afraid of? I guess dread didn't always need a reason.

This is fine. Nothing is wrong. Right?

I told myself again that this wasn't the start of a horror story.

I remembered Anderson once lecturing about 'the mind's ability to create meaning where there is none.' He'd said it with a smirk. Now, I wondered if Anderson had been talking about himself. I wondered whether being up here in the forest alone had warped his mind further.

My phone pinged, showing me I was now a few minutes away from the cabin. I nudged Amelia gently.

"We're nearly there," I told her, gesturing to the windshield. "It's beautiful up here, isn't it?"

She scooted up in her seat, rubbing her eyes as she took in the view.

"It's definitely not London," she muttered, in awe of the wilderness that surrounded us.

74

The trees parted ahead, slowly at first, then wider and wider. Like curtains drawn back on a stage. A field of wildflowers painted the landscape in soft blush pinks and dusky purples. It looked like something from a dream. A beautifully written fairytale, or a meadow providing a false sense of security. Then the cabin finally came into view. A weather-worn refuge that I didn't know I needed until now. I pulled the car to the side and turned off the engine. Neither of us moved. We sat in silence, taking it in.

The cabin was beautiful, built out of heavy timber now darkened by years of rain and moss. The porch wrapped around its frame, like arms around a secret. Strings of large-bulbed fairy lights draped haphazardly from the edge of the roof, waiting for nightfall to bring them to life. I imagined it would look very romantic at night. It was something out of a forgotten fairytale.

We still sat in silence. I wasn't sure if we were admiring the view or avoiding what came next. We shared a nervous smile and simultaneously got out of the car.

The crisp air hit me instantly, waking me up, a welcome slap in the face. The array of rosemary and lavender scents rushed to my lungs. Birds sang in varying tones, cheerful and oblivious. They sang like they didn't know they were being watched. Or maybe they did and sang to drown out the silence. I pulled my bag from the back and slung it over my shoulder. I didn't want to leave. Ever. This was freeing. And yet, something about the air felt too still. The forest was holding its breath.

The light between the trees subtly seemed to shift position. Was it the wind? It wasn't that windy.

I narrowed my gaze deeper into the treeline, trying to get my eyes to adjust to the dancing shadows. This place was a haven, a beautiful sanctuary. And yet, watching the shadows dart past each other just beyond the trees made my stomach turn. I unfocused my eyes and took another deep breath in, making the most of the fresh air.

It is amazing here. I can't let myself be scared of the shadows. No matter how beautiful somewhere or something is, I always find something to be afraid of. I need to start enjoying the peace.

A smile washed over my face as I centred myself.

Amelia met my gaze. "Ready?"

I nodded, unable to hide the large grin that had set on my face. It had been a long time since I had been out of the city. I had almost forgotten what freedom felt like. But as we approached the porch, we both stopped.

The cabin's door was wide open. Wind, maybe. Or Anderson just stepped out for air. Had to be something normal. The feeling of dread sank further into my stomach.

"Do you think he's inside?" I asked, my voice as tight as my chest felt. Amelia paused.

"I sure hope so," she whispered, already uneasy.

Hesitantly, we climbed up the rickety wooden stairs toward the open door. I looked at Amelia, who nodded in agreement as I knocked on the door. The knock echoed around the inside of the cabin, bouncing off every wall and back to me, like the walls had joined in.

No answer.

I raised my fist, ready to knock again. I stopped myself before I touched the wood.

"Should we… just go in?" I asked, my voice falling to a whisper without it meaning to.

I wasn't sure why I was keeping a low volume, but it felt wrong talking at a normal level and disrupting the surrounding peacefulness.

Amelia nodded, "I guess so."

Her voice matched my whispers.

"Professor Anderson? It's me, Amelia. We're coming in!" Her voice was strong and firm, but her body didn't move.

Still nothing.

I decided to step inside first. The air was cool and stale, tinged with damp wood and something else, something faintly metallic.

I dropped my bag onto the old sofa. "Feels empty," I muttered, continuing to look around.

Amelia placed her bag beside mine. "Well, he's clearly not here," she said, but her eyes flicked around nervously.

"Why would he go out and leave the door wide open?" I asked, more out loud to myself than to her.

She hesitated. "Maybe … maybe he felt safe. Maybe there's no one for miles out here."

I peered out of the large window into the sea of trees beyond.

"Isn't he scared something would come inside? Like a bear, or a wolf?" I asked her.

Amelia looked at me and laughed. I didn't understand why she was laughing; I was being deadly serious.

"Lucas, this is still England. There are no bears. There are no wolves. The worst you would get up here is a nosy deer. You're not scared of Bambi, are you?" She teased, nudging my side.

I smirked, but the unease still itched under my skin. Something wasn't right.

I moved through the living room. A mug sat on the table, half-finished coffee, abandoned. Beside it, Anderson's laptop. Dead. Out of charge.

As Amelia searched for the charger, I noticed Anderson's bag sitting by the front door. I made a mental note to check it later.

I walked towards the bedroom door; it was already ajar. As I pushed it fully open, the first thing I noticed was the flower paintings on the walls, and an unmade single bed. Lived in and cozy. I came out of the bedroom and spotted the bathroom. As I reached the doorway, I paused. The air felt…colder. Not brisk, but wrong. Like walking through someone else's breath. The floor was still glistening slightly. Wet. The towel lay in a crumpled heap beside the sink. *Sloppy*, I thought. Not like the Anderson I know. I walked further into the room, passing the cabinet mirror. The floor was sticky underfoot. A tacky pull with every cautious step. I paused and double-took the reflection. In my peripheral vision, I saw the adjacent window open in the mirror. I turned towards it. It was closed. Were my eyes now playing tricks on me? I could have been sure it was open in the reflection. Maybe I just saw it wrong. Mirrors can distort. Can't they? They blend light. That's all it was. A trick of the mirror, that's all… But then, why did I feel like the room had shifted around me?

Then I saw it, a smear on the white bathroom tiles. A red mark. Blood?

My eyes continued down the wall to the floor. More red droplets. I turned on myself and followed them back out into the living room,

78

to the foot of the table. Had Anderson hurt himself? He was obviously okay enough to get up and leave because, well; he wasn't here. But then, where was he and what if we're too late?

He may have a concussion. Depending on how bad the fall was, he could have passed out somewhere in the forest. Alone. I knew we should go out there and try to find him. This could be how people disappear, all those missing people that just vanish. Do the people that look for them end up missing too? I swallowed down the thought. Amelia noticed what I was looking at.

"Is that... blood?" She asked, having caught up behind me. Her words startled me. I shook off the feeling of dread quickly and focused on the matter at hand. I crouched down.

"Yeah. I think he may have slipped." I studied the droplets.

Her hand flew to her mouth. "Oh, my god..."

"Maybe he went to find help. Or to find a doctor," I said, my mind running through rational explanations, but the words sounded thinner than expected.

"Yeah...maybe," Amelia said, but her voice lacked conviction.

A damp, sour scent hung thick in the air. Not just mould, something organic. Something wrong. It crawled into my sinuses like damp fur. The walls were too quiet. As if they'd been holding their breath since we had walked through the front door.

We stood and stared at the crimson blotches. She didn't speak. Neither did I. The air felt heavier now, like the cabin itself was listening.

A sound creaked overhead, like the sound of someone creeping over old floorboards. We both looked at each other, frozen.

"Someone's upstairs," I stated, my tone flat.

Amelia exhaled and tried to smile at me, although her lips wouldn't allow more than a slight smirk.

"Lucas, there is no upstairs, it's probably just an old, creaky roof," she told me, walking back towards the front door.

She opened the door and stepped onto the porch, scanning the ground as if she were searching for breadcrumbs. A trail. Anything.

Nothing.

She looked up towards the edge of the forest.

"But… if he left to get help, why is his car still parked outside?"

I joined her on the porch. Anderson's car sat silently in the clearing, its windows fogged slightly. I didn't know why I hadn't noticed it before. Maybe I had and dismissed it as normal, as I expected him to be here. But there it was, sitting there in all its glory. Abandoned.

The sound came again, but this time it wasn't so much of a creak. It sounded like tapping. Rhythmical tapping. Like nails on glass.

There is no one around. It's old pipes, or just old cabin noises. There's no one else here. I told myself.

The birds stopped tweeting. All at once. As if someone had pressed mute on the forest. Then they chirped back, just a little too eagerly, like actors trying to cover a missed cue.

A small robin perched on the railing of the porch in front of us. It was still, too still. Its wings didn't twitch. And it didn't blink. Can birds blink? Its head tilted to one side, not curious, but deliberate. Like a dog listening to a command. I felt a sudden urge to wave my hand, just to see if it would mimic the motion. The bird didn't move. Like it knew we were watching. It wanted us to know. As if it could hear my thoughts, it took off back into the treeline.

We both walked over to the porch rail where the bird had just fled, and leant up against it, staring into the woods. A chill ran up my spine, nerves prickling like they'd just been jolted awake. I wasn't sure if it was because my arm had just brushed Amelia's, or if it was the feeling of not being the only ones here. The wind picked up, causing the trees to rustle and whisper amongst themselves, as if they were trying to speak.

For the first time since arriving, the forest no longer looked beautiful.

It looked like it was watching.

Chapter 8

Amelia

I didn't know what conclusion to come to or even how to come to one. Where had Anderson gone? If he had, in fact, fallen in the bathroom and then left the cabin, he could be concussed and confused. But surely, if he had gone to look for help, he would have cleaned up the blood first or even called someone. And even if he had, that still didn't explain the email. My thoughts were spiralling, twisting into knots that made my stomach turn. I was confused, overwhelmed, and my head was spinning with endless possibilities of what had happened and where he had gone.

I turned to Lucas, hoping he would offer something solid. Something comforting. A theory that felt less like a horror novel and more like something grounded in real life. But he just stared back at me, wearing the same expression I knew was mirrored on my own face: uncertain, wide-eyed, unsettled.

Eventually, after what felt like forever, Lucas moved. He took a slow breath, then turned toward the kitchen.

"Where are you going?" I asked, my voice too sharp, too quick. I didn't know what to do, I just knew I didn't want to be alone right now.

"I'm going to grab a coffee," he said simply, already filling the kettle. "You want one?"

The tapping of the old plumbing and the hiss of water as it escaped echoed through the cabin, like hammer strikes to my temples. I flinched. I needed silence, space to think.

"How can you be so calm?" I snapped. "How can you just sit and drink a coffee like we're not in the middle of a crisis?"

I really didn't understand how his brain worked sometimes. His calmness made me more anxious. Lucas turned to me slowly.

"Because, Mils, if I let myself spiral, it won't help either of us. I could go running into the forest, shouting his name, freaking out. I want to. But right now, you need me. We need to stay calm. For him. For us. We don't know what state he'll be in when we find him—because we will find him."

I watched as he opened his arms, the invitation was clear.

I didn't hesitate. I stepped forward and folded into his embrace, wrapping my arms around his waist and burying my head in his chest.

The weight of his hug instantly calmed me, and I relaxed into him. If I closed my eyes and forgot where I was and why I was here, I could have stayed in his arms forever.

I used to mock his calmness, never being able to understand how he stayed so level-headed in times of stress like exams or tension between friends. Now, I was more thankful for it than ever. He helped my head stop spinning; my thoughts stop racing. *Had I become more dependent on him than I realised?*

"Thank you," I whispered, slowly releasing my grip from around him. "Thank you for always being there. For being here now."

Lucas pressed a kiss to the top of my head. "I'll always be here for you, Mils."

I felt the temperature in my cheeks rise as he drew me back in tighter.

"Don't you think we should call the police or something?" I asked, not really sure what our next steps should be, but knowing I don't think we can deal with this alone. Lucas stood in silence for a moment, pondering our options.

"No, not yet. I just have a gut feeling. Plus, I don't want them to think he's insane. We should see if we can find him first," he finally said.

A pang of cold hit my stomach. That answer didn't sit quite right with me. We aren't trained professionals, and we don't know how to navigate a forest and search for someone. But Lucas had dealt with this sort of thing before, he must be doing what he thinks is best for Anderson. I let my body relax into him.

We stood together, arms around each other until the kettle began its shrill and relentless whistle.

I went to sit in the front room of the cabin whilst Lucas fumbled about in the kitchen. I pulled my phone out to drop Charlie a message telling her we had got here safe and asking if Snowy was being a good boy and then shoved my phone back into my pocket. Sinking into the sofa and quickly discovered it wasn't as comfortable as it looked, I stared out the big window in front of me. I focused on the slight cracks in the corners, the swaying branches just beyond the cabin, the greying sky, the swaying grass. The buzz in my pocket drew me from my focus, I pulled out my phone. Charlie had replied.

'I'm glad to hear it. Yes, he's being a good by. Is Lucas?'

She ended the message with a pair of eye emojis. I rolled my eyes and sent her back the corresponding emoji in response and placed my phone on the coffee table.

After a few hours of pacing, pondering, and going around in circles, figuratively and literally, I was glued to my laptop. The Wi-Fi connection was dropping in and out. I was cross-referencing maps, reading blog posts about the area, trying to find something, anything, that might offer some clue to where Anderson had gone. Missing person reports. Mental health first-aid articles. Forest ranger protocols. The kind of desperate Googling someone does when reason is fading and all that's left is the hope that answers live online. I jumped at the sudden sound of the walls rattling; the wind had gotten stronger. I shivered and looked around for Lucas. He was deep into his third family-sized bag of crisps, clicking through cupboards in search of actual food.

"Can you check if he had anything edible here?" I asked him, looking back down at my laptop. "I'm starving."

Lucas looked around. "Yeah, sure," he said, mouth full of salt and vinegar crisps. "Have you checked if his laptop's alive yet?"

"Oh god!" I said, suddenly remembering.

I leapt off the sofa, rushing over to the table. I tapped the laptop's power button. After a few password guesses, I finally typed in *Password1!* and let out a laugh. Typical.

"What's funny?" Lucas called, rustling through cans of soup and decades-old noodles.

"Nothing," I replied with a grin. "I'm in."

Outside, the wind picked up again, rattling the window frames like skeletal fingers. Another shiver ran down my spine. The laptop was sluggish; because of course it was. I tried connecting to the internet, failed, and then tried to hotspot it from my phone.

"It really doesn't like the internet here," I muttered, picking the laptop up and holding it closer to the sky.

Lucas, boiling two chicken and mushroom pot noodles, rolled his eyes at my attempt to get closer to the Wi-Fi via air.

"You know that doesn't work, right?" he chuckled. "That machine's basically a fossil, anyway. I'm surprised it can even run a browser."

I zoned out at his ever so helpful explanation and looked through Anderson's tabs and open apps. His email inbox showed mine to be the last message he'd sent. His research doc was open, half-finished, mostly notes about microclimates, animal behavioural changes, and some erratic speculation. I frowned. It was nice to see he kept to his studies whilst he was up here on his own, but it seemed a little… obsessive, from what I was reading.

"He was doing some research," I called to Lucas.

He came over, noodles in hand, and sat beside me.

"Anything interesting?"

I scrolled down. "I'm not sure, it's going to take me some time to read through all these notes. They're not very organised."

As I tried to continue reading, Lucas distracted me as he attempted to cool the noodles by blowing on them and then immediately burnt his tongue.

"Do you ever stop eating?"

"Never," he mumbled, mouth full.

Bang.

The sudden noise shook the entire cabin. We both froze. Hearts pounding. Holding our breath.

The sound of the door slamming against the inside wall echoed through the cabin.

Our heads snapped toward the noise. Silence.

Just the wind.

I let out a sigh of relief as the door continued to bang against the inside wall. Clearly locking the doors here was a necessity if you wanted to keep the wind from inviting itself in.

I walked over to the door and closed it, bolting it shut. I turned and gave Lucas a weak smile. We both laughed, but it wasn't genuine. Not really.

I needed to decompress. Everything felt a little too claustrophobic inside that cabin. The silence, the unanswered questions, the smell of damp wood. It was all weighing on me.

I paused for a moment, thinking about whether what I was about to suggest was a smart idea. I guessed it was as good an idea as any.

"Let's go for a walk," I suggested. "Just the perimeter. Around the trees."

Lucas nodded. "Yeah. Might help us clear our heads."

I wasn't very happy with my idea, but it was the only thing I could think of to release my nervous energy. I found a spare key to the cabin within a few minutes of looking in a few living room drawers. We put on our hoodies and stepped outside, locking the door behind us.

"Do you think the wind blew the door open when we arrived?" I asked as we stepped into the trees. The wet mud squelched beneath my boots, causing me to lose my footing. I steadied myself as we continued.

"Maybe," Lucas replied, hands in his pockets. "But it wasn't windy this morning."

"So… you think maybe he left last night?" I asked quietly.

"I-I don't know." he said, truthfully. "I hope not."

We walked side by side. I instinctively began twirling my hair around my fingers. Partly to stop the wind from blowing it in my face, partly habit.

A fox stood still on the trail ahead, its head low, eyes fixed. It didn't run. It didn't blink. It just stared at us until Lucas made a sound, and then it disappeared like mist.

The wind howled through the trees, sharp as a distant scream. The surrounding forest creaked and sighed. Fallen leaves clung to our boots. The scent of rotting bark and damp moss clung to everything. Despite the haunting atmosphere, I found something comforting in the forest. There was a rhythm to it, the rustle of leaves, the sway of branches, the squelch of soil. Even the oppressive quiet had a strange sort of lull to it.

Lucas kept pointing out oddly shaped tree trunks and abandoned bird nests. He seemed to be genuinely enjoying himself. It was easy to be overcome by the beauty of the place, before the real reason we were trudging through the woods came back to mind.

"It's so beautiful out here," he said, looking up at the treetops, eyes wide like a kid.

"It's cold and wet," I said, "but… yeah. I guess it is kind of nice." I carefully stepped over a fallen tree trunk, ensuring I wouldn't lose my footing to the wet mud. The forest fascinated him. Had he never been to one before? Or can he see something I can't?

I wasn't sure he'd even heard me. He was already a few steps ahead, admiring a curved birch that looked like a question mark.

My shadow leaned sideways across the tree trunk, even though the sun was behind me. I stepped back instinctively. Just light trickery… probably.

Something off to the right took my attention. I stopped and squinted, trying to see between the trees and mist. There was another trail, snapped branches and old leaves moved aside. In the middle of the trail I could see something shining, something reflective. I turned back to Lucas, who was still mesmerised by the question mark tree. Quickly, I trudged over the mud and branches, pulling myself over another fallen trunk. I walked towards the object and bent down to pick it up. A flock of birds erupted from the trees, causing my heart to jolt at the sudden disturbance. I examined the object in my hand. It was

90

a small, thick piece of glass. From someone's glasses? Had someone else been up here recently?

I recalled the last time I had seen Anderson with his thick-rimmed glasses. Were they his?

The wind erupted into howls, almost knocking me off balance. I looked back over to Lucas, who had seemed to get bored with the strangely shaped tree and had continued up the path. I dropped the glass back on the floor and hurried back over to catch up with him.

"Lucas, wait!" I shouted, but he couldn't hear me through the wind.

I managed to get back to where I had been and stopped to catch my breath, keeping Lucas in my eye-line. I watched him walk a little ahead, just out of reach. The thought struck me hard: what if I turned, and he was gone? Not in a dramatic way. Just… gone. Like Anderson. Like the forest had chosen him.

The trees seemed to shift. The wind must have been strong today, because the thick branches hit each other with a bang. Shadows flickered beyond them. The wet, damp forest smell lingered around me, combining mould and something… *metallic?* Then everything stopped, like someone turning a fan off; the wind halted. But the trees bowed right. I froze, watching the leaves shift in a way that defied the air's pull. My breath caught in my throat. Don't imagine things, I told myself. Don't give the forest more than it is.

I remembered being ten years old, stuck in the school woods during a camping trip. The teacher's whistle never reached me. The stillness had crept under my skin then too, just like now. I lingered for a moment, turning back towards the cabin, barely visible now between the trees. The path behind us no longer looked like the one we came from. Were the trees closer than before?

I felt it then: a strange shift in the atmosphere.

The kind of shift you feel when the universe is telling you nothing will ever be the same again.

The kind of shift you feel when someone's standing right behind you and the small, icy chills crawl slowly up your stiff spine.

Like you're being watched.

Chapter 9

Lucas

I couldn't get enough of this forest. It was everything I'd dreamed about. The peace. The sounds. The smell of the moss and bark. The way the trees reached up into the grey, bruised sky. The way the light bled through the canopy was like ink in water. It was perfect. Everything was so immersive, all I could focus on was the nature. Nothing else around me fazed me. Like noise-cancelling headphones, everything else was muted.

As I climbed up the path, I almost forgot Amelia was even behind me. Reality caught up with me, and I shook myself out of my daze. A twinge of guilt sank to the bottom of my stomach, and I could feel my face growing hotter. How could I have forgotten that Amelia was behind me? Yes, the forest was captivating, but it wasn't more captivating than she was. Even though the beauty overwhelmed me, I still couldn't shake the unease that looking beyond the treeline, and deeper into the forest gave me. There was nothing out here apart from me, Amelia, and a plethora of different small animals — that's all.

I brushed my shaggy hair from my face as I turned back towards her, waiting for her to catch up.

A faint noise sang to me from between the branches. Was that a voice?

My mind flipped from Amelia to the enticing sound that whispered to me through the canopy of branches. I squinted my eyes and tried to stare deep into the treeline, cupping my hands over my eyes to block the stray sunlight.

Nothing.

And then came the sound again. Just a gentle sound. Could it have been?

"Hey, hold up!" Amelia called out, trying to match my pace.

Her voice came back into focus in my mind. I turned and waited but felt a twitch of irritation stir in my chest. I didn't mean to feel that way, not toward her, but there was so much more to explore, and so little time.

Where was that sound coming from?

Every part of me felt magnetically pulled forward. I didn't want to keep stopping.

"What's going on with you? What's the rush?" She panted as she finally caught up, her cheeks flushed from the effort.

I didn't know how to answer. What was the rush? I didn't know. I just… needed to keep moving. It felt right. Like I'd lose something if I stopped. It wasn't adrenaline. It wasn't curiosity. It was something older, more primal. Like something was pulling me forward, threading

94

urgency into my bloodstream. A sound, or a silence, that pulled at the marrow. Something deep in my bones itched to press on. It reminded me of something I couldn't quite place. A dream, maybe. A nightmare? I wasn't sure. But I'd felt this before. Maybe not in this lifetime. But somewhere.

"Sorry," I muttered finally. A cold wetness clung to my face as I realised it had started to pour with rain. The sloppy mud and decaying leaves mixed with the rain to create a concoction of earthy Autumn scents that hit me all at once. I don't know how long it had been raining for, but when I took a good look at Amelia, she was drenched.

She stood still beside me for a moment, trying to catch her breath. My legs twitched, ready to keep going. The restlessness in my chest was spreading. I wanted to keep walking, but she was slowing me down. Weighing me down.

What the hell is wrong with me?

When we'd arrived at the cabin just hours ago, all I'd wanted was to be alone with her. Now, suddenly, I couldn't stand still. I didn't want to be near anyone. Not even her.

I could feel her confusion as she looked up at me, her brows drawn with concern. My behaviour wasn't making sense. Even to me.

"Lucas, I'm cold, and I'm wet, and I'm exhausted," she breathed, her voice shaking with weariness.

I didn't answer. I stood there silently, locked in place. Tiredness was not something I felt. Actually, I felt more awake than I had in weeks, as if caffeine had replaced my blood.

"Lucas," she repeated, her voice quieter now, more fragile. "Are you listening to me? It's going to get dark really soon…can we please go back?"

Her words echoed in my head like a distant radio. Muffled. Fuzzy. My ears were buzzing. My whole body was pulsing with the need to move.

"Lucas!" she shouted this time.

That snapped me out of it.

"I'm sorry," I said quickly, rubbing the back of my neck. "I don't know what came over me. You're right. Of course, you're right. Let's go back."

She exhaled and smiled faintly, relieved. She reached for my hand, and this time, I didn't pull away. We walked back together, hand in hand. But as much as I tried to focus on the walk back, on the beautiful girl walking alongside me, something niggled in my chest. A pull that took all my strength to ignore.

The walk back felt a lot faster than I thought it would be, a lot easier. As we reached the porch, I noticed muddy boot prints up the stairs towards the front door of the cabin. The rain had almost washed them away, but they were still visible.

My heart pounded and sank simultaneously. Were they there before? Could it have been Anderson trying to come back? I looked back at Amelia; her face was tight with irritation and cold. Opening my mouth to tell Amelia what I could see, I found myself speechless. I swallowed my words and turned back around. Choosing to remain silent, I didn't mention the boot prints to her. I didn't want to freak her out or annoy her anymore. And anyway, they were probably from us before.

I unlocked the door and stepped into the warmth of the cabin. Amelia followed closely, drenched and muddy. She kicked off her boots, and I did the same, mirroring her motions.

"What happened out there?" she asked, her voice soft but probing. She was watching me carefully now, as if waiting for some unknown thing to crawl out of me.

"I'm not sure," I said after a pause. "Maybe it's the stress. Maybe it's everything finally catching up with me. I just wanted to keep walking. It felt peaceful. Being out there. Amongst all the nothing."

In truth, I did not know why it felt so impossible to stop walking. The silence out there didn't soothe me; it called to me. Whispered. It felt as if I had stopped too soon, something would've caught up to me.

"I understand," Amelia whispered. She walked over and took my hands, grounding me. "It's been a lot. On both of us."

I watched her gaze drift to the window. The trees were dark silhouettes now, swaying in the wind. The drizzle hadn't stopped. A heavy grey sky had swallowed what was left of the day.

She let go of me and disappeared toward the bathroom. I didn't move at first, then I wandered towards the living room window. I stood there, hands in my pockets, staring blankly out into the woods.

"What are we going to do about Anderson?" Amelia's voice broke into my thoughts. "It's dark now... I don't think he's coming back tonight."

I blinked. How long had she been standing there? Minutes? Hours?

I pressed my forehead against the cold window glass. My breath fogged the pane, obscuring the trees. Maybe it wasn't just the forest. Maybe something inside *me* had shifted.

It felt like my legs would collapse if I had stopped walking earlier. The thought scared me, that and the fact Amelia's voice had sounded so far away. I blinked hard, gripping the windowsill. It was just stress. It had to be. I'd felt this kind of thing before… hadn't I?

My gaze shifted from the treeline outside the window and turned towards Amelia. I couldn't even remember it getting completely pitch black out there.

"I don't think we can do anything until morning," I said finally. "Police won't act until the forty-eight-hour mark, and it's too late to drive back tonight. We'll sleep. Then we'll go."

"You're right," she mumbled. "We just… wait, I guess. What about sleeping arrangements?"

I turned from the window, forcing a smile. "I'll take the sofa. You take the bed."

She looked at the floor, twisting a strand of hair between her fingers.

"Would you rather have the sofa?" I teased lightly.

She shook her head. "No, I just…I don't want to be alone right now."

I felt my face getting hotter as I stepped towards her.

"You're not alone," I whispered.

She met my eyes, her expression softening.

"I was actually going to suggest we share the bed," I added with a smile, pulling her into a hug.

She giggled, her forehead pressing against my chest. "You just want the warm side."

I grinned. "You know me too well."

We held onto each other longer than necessary. Neither of us seemed ready to pull away.

The bed was small, but it didn't feel cramped. We lay facing each other, tucked under the blanket. The faint silver glow of the moon leaked through the edge of the curtains, casting streaks of pale light across the wall.

Amelia drew small circles on my chest with her finger. My hand found the small of her back, resting there naturally.

The wind and rain hurled outside the window, causing the walls to shake and creak. But in bed with her, I felt safe.

"Thank you again," she whispered. " I wouldn't be able to do this alone."

I tucked a stray hair behind her ear. "Of course. You're stuck with me now."

She looked up at me, her expression unreadable. Her eyes were wide, but not with fear. I thought I saw something else flicker there. Something I hadn't seen before. Had she finally stopped seeing me as just her best friend?

"I mean, if I hadn't come, who would've made your terrible pot noodles?" I added with a laugh, trying to diffuse the moment.

She didn't laugh.

Instead, she leaned forward, grasping the back of my head, entangling her fingers in my hair. She pulled my head towards hers. Our eyes were fixed on one another, staring deeply. Just looking at each other. Then her lips touched mine in a hungered frenzy. Her grip on my hair tightened as she deepened her kiss. My lips moved with hers, desperate. Urgent. The world fell silent. No wind, no rain, no creaking. A silence almost too complete, like the cabin had been vacuum sealed. Just my own heart pounding. Everything in me ignited. I had wanted this for so long. It felt so surreal, but so right. It frightened me and excited me all at once. My heart raced as her soft lips brushed across mine. I wrapped one hand in the back of her hair and the other on the silky skin of her lower back, pulling her closer to me.

Tingles washed down my back as her tongue danced around mine, ever so softly. My grasp on her body became tighter as I pulled her on top of me. Her weight grounded me to the mattress as we lost ourselves in each other. Our bodies pressed together heatedly; our breaths became synchronised.

She ran her hand up my body, taking my T-shirt with it. She stopped just as she had pulled it up to my chest. She stopped there for a moment, her hands lingering on me, her eyes fixed on mine. For a second, I wished the world would stop turning. She tugged back on my T-shirt. Just as her fingers began to remove it —

Bang.

We froze.

A loud crash rattled the outside wall. The sound too loud and too heavy for glass, but it came from the window. Amelia pulled away and sat up, her chest rising and falling. Her gaze shot to the window. Her breath hitched. She twisted her head, eyes wide. I followed her gaze.

"Did you see that?" she whispered. Her hand inched toward the curtain. I caught her wrist.

"No," I said too quickly. I tried to slow my breathing so she wouldn't know how fast my heart was beating.

She looked at me, not afraid of me, but afraid of what she might see. She was about to speak again when another bang hit the wall like a gunshot. This time, closer. Neither of us moved. Her hand dropped. The hairs on my arms stood on end, chills scattering between them. The moonlight that had once glowed through the gap in the curtain was gone. Ripped away and replaced with darkness. Pitch black.

"…Does the moon just disappear like that?" I asked, barely above a whisper.

"I think," her voice caught in her throat, her eyes wide with shock. "I think something's out there."

"It was probably just the wind again," I whispered, trying to mask my frustration at whatever had rudely interrupted the moment. But the frustration didn't last long, as another noise came from outside the cabin. It was smaller and softer than before. *A footstep maybe?* Then, a shadow. A long, tall shadow. It engulfed the entire window, blocking all light from outside. That was no cloud; something was out there. Then, movement. Something moved from behind the window. I was sure of it. Something or someone was out there. It couldn't be Anderson. No. Actually, it couldn't be human. The shadow was too tall. And it couldn't be a tree branch; there was no movement, it didn't sway in the wind. It was just still. The darkness felt thick, as if something had pressed its body against the window.

"Shall I have a look?" Amelia said, her voice so thin as if she's trying not to be heard.

I lifted a finger to her lips and shook my head. My gut was telling me not to move, not to look. I was more than happy to run with that right now. Her hands shook as she placed them on my finger.

Bang.

This one was louder now. It vibrated though the cabin with such force that I tightened my grip on Amelia. A cold burst of air flew around the room and bit at my ankles, like something had exhaled against my skin. I couldn't move to cover them; I couldn't move at all.

Neither of us could. We both held our breath. The windowsill groaned as if something were leaning on it. A crack, as if the weight was too much for it to bear. Then it started again.

The banging continued on and off. In a rhythm. Three bangs — pause —— three bangs. Like a terrifying metronome. But the pause was too long; each time it felt like it was getting longer, like it was waiting for a response. Trying to slow my breath, I became very aware of how tight my hands were grasped on her hips, I let go of her and glanced toward the window.

A small slither of moonlight shot through the curtains. I twisted my head back quickly as if the moonlight would show whatever was out there that I was looking. It didn't make sense, but none of this made sense. It wasn't enough moonlight to make a difference, not enough to see what was outside. But enough to know whatever was out there was moving. My breath caught, I felt my heart beating in my throat.

I slowly, carefully guided Amelia to lie down beside me again, though we both remained stiff and scared.

I had never truly known the feeling of being watched. But now that I had, I never wanted to feel it again.

Not ever.

I used to think fear looked like flashing lights and loud sirens. But this? This was quiet. Heavy. Like something ancient pressing into my chest. I didn't know if it was the woods or myself unravelling.

We stayed like that. Arms wrapped around one another. Not daring to speak. Not daring to move. The banging became softer, as if reacting to my lowering heartbeat. The same rhythm, but less intense. Eventually, after what felt like hours, the banging stopped. And the wind and rain started again. We stayed still.

What would have happened if I had gotten up and looked outside? What would I have seen?

With my heart pounding, my head not knowing what to do, I lay there frozen in fear.

I tried to count the seconds in the silence as the wind returned to the forest. The rain came back too, but differently this time. The taps of raindrops were slower, more rhythmic.

I closed my eyes and focused on my breath, trying to ground myself until the sun could greet me with safety.

Chapter 10

Amelia

I was woken by the rising sun peeking through the curtains, soft and golden. It streaked across the room in warm lines that painted my face and made shadows dance on the walls. It should have felt peaceful, but the beautiful morning now reminded me of the calm before a storm.

I didn't know how I was able to sleep after what happened last night, but maybe being terrified had simply worn me out. I rolled and glanced at Lucas who was still asleep, his chest gently rising and falling, his expression peaceful. Tightness pooled in my chest at the sight of him, so innocent and delicate.

I lay there a moment longer, thoughts swirling, refusing to let my mind rest. What could have been outside the window last night? My mind clung to the unknown. Was it Anderson? Some kind of animal? Something more sinister? My stomach turned as my imagination took control. I shook my head, pushing the thoughts away, reminding myself

I didn't believe in ghosts or the supernatural. Still, the feeling of dread lingered just beneath my skin.

The memories of the shadow still clung to me, and beneath that, guilt. For the kiss. A wave of embarrassment suddenly flushed over me as last night's events replayed in my mind. My cheeks grew hot. What had come over me?

I had always thought Lucas was cute, more than cute, and had let the idea of "more than just friends" wander into my mind from time to time. But I had never acted on it. Not after his mum passed, he had already lost so much. If it didn't work out between us, then who would he be left with? No one.

I remembered the first day I had met him; he had helped me with my boxes that I had dropped when moving dorms. I remembered my cheeks growing hotter as he lifted my boxes up one-handed, flashing me a cheeky grin. I had liked him ever since and had hoped something would happen between us. But now I knew he just needed a friend more than anything, and that was more important.

I looked at Lucas again, still deep in his slumber; my heart tugged. Lying beside him should have brought comfort, but all I felt now was confusion. I had always thought the way he frowned in his sleep was cute. I had watched him sleep multiple times. When he drifted off halfway through our movie marathons, he always looked so peaceful when he was sleeping. Like nothing could hurt him.

Knowing that spiralling in my thoughts would only make things worse, I slid carefully out of the bed, trying not to wake him. Barefoot and quiet, I tiptoed towards the bathroom.

Careful to close the door behind me and not wake Lucas, I took a deep breath in. Finally, I was alone and able to think. Throwing my hair up into a messy bun, I flicked on the water for the shower. Steam began curling into the air as the water sprinkled across the tiled floor. I opened the cabinet and began scanning the bottles, hands moving quickly as my chest tightened. *Something calming… anything.* I settled on a bottle of rose essential oil and stepped into the shower.

The hot water poured over my skin, but I didn't react. I stood still, the heat rushing past my ears like static, the sound of it dull and far away. I poured the oil into my palm and rubbed it over my arms, willing the scent to seep into me. The soft aroma of rose filled the air like velvet, but even that couldn't soothe the ache now tightening in my throat.

My breathing quickened. I pressed my hand to my mouth to stifle the sob that escaped. Another followed. Tears ran down my cheeks and mixed with the shower's stream as my body shook. My legs gave way, and I sank down slowly, folding myself at the bottom of the shower. The cold porcelain bit at my thighs. The scent of rose oil clung to the steam, now too sweet. My mind spiralled with the thought of Lucas's hand on my hips, his soft lips against mine, his dissociation in the forest, the shadow.

The water wasn't washing me clean; it was spreading panic instead. My sobs echoed in the small space. Deep breaths came in broken waves between cries.

I recalled my mum's advice during my panic attacks. Say five things you can see, hear, feel, and smell. I sat there, counting colours and objects around the room, letting the water pour over me like a cleansing storm. As if it could carry away the chaos inside.

Time slipped by unnoticed. I wasn't sure how long I'd been sitting there, but by the time my mind returned to the moment, the water had turned from hot to lukewarm, and now to nearly ice-cold. My skin was goose-pimpled, but I barely felt it. The numbness was stronger.

I blinked myself out of the trance, turned off the shower, and reached for a towel. Wrapping it around me tightly, I stepped in front of the mirror. My reflection stared back: flushed cheeks, red-rimmed eyes, hair damp and curled around my face. I looked… tired. Not just tired. Broken.

I splashed cold water over my cheeks, hoping it might shock the sadness out of me. *You're stronger than this.* I usually was, but this time was different. A missing professor. A haunting message. A kiss that didn't feel like a mistake, and the terrifying figure beyond the glass.

I felt so selfish. I wasn't here for romance or excitement; I was here to find my professor. To find a missing person.

My thoughts took me back to last night. I couldn't shake the image of that shadow. Too still to be wind, too tall to be an animal. My mind filled in the rest, and none of it was good.

I let out a small, breathless laugh. It sounded strange in the bathroom's silence. I was certain that one day we'd look back on all this and laugh, awkwardly maybe, but laugh, nonetheless. Once we found Anderson. Once everything had calmed down.

I sighed, pulled on my clothes, and walked back into the living room.

I collapsed onto the sofa, staring out the window at the delicate morning sun. The birds were tweeting; the ground was warming. It was my favourite time of day, a time I would usually feel happiest, excited for the day ahead. Now, dread had consumed me. The light wind outside grazing the cabin walls was peaceful, but the light creaking from the rafters felt unsettling. Then, something beyond the glass caught my eye. I noticed something standing just beyond the tree line, slightly too hidden by the trees to make out what it was. I got up and walked over to the window, trying to focus my eyes softly to see through the gentle shadows the trees were casting.

A deer. It was just standing there, staring at me. It was so still. Its ears didn't twitch. It wasn't even blinking. I stared back at it. Was something wrong? Was it hurt?

Something about it didn't feel right; that feeling twisted in my stomach. Its body was still, yes, but too still. Not the typical 'frozen in headlights' look a deer gives, more like a mannequin, like taxidermy. Its head was tilted slightly to one side, like it was listening. The wind swayed the surrounding branches, but its fur remained stuck.

The creak of the bedroom door opening wavered my attention, and I glanced towards the noise. It was Lucas, shuffling slowly into the room, still sleepy. I had turned my head for a second, barely a blink, and when I looked again, the deer was gone. The trees remained untouched. Not a single branch swayed.

I turned back towards Lucas. When I saw him, my chest tightened, warmth rising sharply to my throat. I swallowed it down, wiping my damp palms against my jeans.

His hair was a fluffy mess, tousled from sleep, and his shirt, a little too tight, clung to his chest and arms in all the right places, carefree. His goofy Labrador smile made my heart hurt more than it should have.

"Morning, beautiful!" he said with a wide grin, walking over to greet me.

He stepped towards me, leaning in for a kiss. Without thinking, I placed my hand gently on his chest and stepped back.

"Oh. I'm, I'm sorry. I…" he stammered, smile faltering into confusion and a touch of embarrassment.

"No, no — I'm sorry…" I said quickly, a twist of guilt forming in my stomach. I should have let him kiss me. I wanted to. Everything in my body pulled towards him, gravitated towards his touch, but I resisted.

"No, it's fine. I get it. I'm sorry," he muttered, taking a step back, his eyes dropping to the floor.

"It's not you, it's just…" I began, trying to untangle my words without hurting him. "I don't want to mess this up. Our friendship. I think it would get complicated, and I don't want to lose you."

"Yeah. I get it. It was situational. We're friends. A mistake. I get it," he said, still not looking up.

I winced. Was this worse than if I had just kissed him back? My heart ached. I reached for his hand.

"Lucas, please. It's not that I don't care. I do. I just can't do this right now, not here. Not with Anderson missing, and whatever happened outside that window. It's just too much."

He didn't just nod, he dragged his hand away from mine. His face twisted, not in anger, but in something worse. Sadness. "I feel the same. It was just… last night. It was nice."

"It was nice," I echoed. "But maybe we can talk about this later? Once we've found Anderson. Once we're out of this… mess."

I gestured around us, half-laughing. I tried, with all the strength I could find, to give him a comforting smile, but my lips wouldn't allow it.

"Yeah. I get it," he said, a smile barely tugging at the corners of his mouth. "Doesn't make it any easier."

We both stood there in the awkward silence, Lucas staring at the floor, me staring at him. I wanted him to say something, anything. But I knew there was nothing more left to be said.

"I'm gonna get dressed, then we can head to the police station, yeah?" he said, breaking the tension, already turning towards the bedroom.

I parted my lips to take it all back. To tell him I was doing this for his sake, that I actually wanted this. But I pulled myself back into reality; it wasn't a good idea.

"Sure," my voice was weak, and the guilt didn't let go.

Lucas disappeared into the bedroom, and the shadow of the doorway swallowed him whole. I collapsed into the dent I'd left in the sofa before. The cushions were still warm from my body. My heart thudded. What was I doing?

I twirled a lock of my wet hair around my fingers. I liked Lucas. Maybe even more. And every part of me wanted to run into the bedroom, wrap my arms around him, and never let go. But I couldn't.

Not now. Not when Anderson was still missing. Not when the air still felt thick with something unknown.

I wanted to message Charlie. To vent to someone else other than my mind. However, I knew she would meet it with girlish excitement instead of the creeping dread and regret I felt. I decided it was best to keep this from her for now.

Priorities. That's why we came here, to find answers. Not to cloud my mind with selfish desires.

But no matter how many times I told myself that, the ache in my stomach didn't leave.

The twinge of guilt curled inside me like a knot. I didn't want to hurt him. And yet, that's exactly what I had done.

I wanted to call him back. Tell him I was frightened, not that I lacked interest. It had all felt too real. My fingers gripped the edge of the sofa as if it might anchor me in place, stop me from following him into the bedroom.

When we find Anderson, I'll tell Lucas how I really feel.

Chapter 11

Lucas

We both jumped into the car in silence. Neither of us spoke while getting ready to go. Now, even seated side-by-side, it was as though an invisible wall had wedged itself between us. The silence wasn't just quiet; it was awkward. Heavy with unspoken thoughts.

Outside, the forest was slowly brightening. The sun broke through the canopy, warming the cool morning air. Dappled rays stretched across the road like golden fingers. The trees, with their mossy trunks and yellowed leaves, lined the edges of the narrow path, while birds chirped somewhere up high, unseen.

I tightened my grip on the steering wheel.

Just focus on driving.

I flicked my eyes to my left, stealing a quick glance at Amelia beside me. She was looking straight ahead, eyes wide and slightly distant, twirling a piece of her hair. She didn't look at me, not even once. I had known that words can hurt; I had learnt that from a young age, but I had never realised before that silence could hurt much more.

Does she feel as awkward as I do?

My thoughts circled back to the night before. She had kissed me. It wasn't tentative. It was certain. It was intentional. But this morning, she wouldn't even meet my gaze. I understood why she wanted to stay friends, if something went wrong between us, then they may never be as close again. I didn't want that either. But I wouldn't let it get to that. I would never allow myself to lose her, no matter what.

Was she embarrassed? Or was it something else entirely?

I wanted to ask her. Desperately, but instead, I just kept driving.

I remembered our first road trip to Brighton last spring. With the windows down, music too loud, Amelia's laughter filled the car like sunlight. Now, the silence between us was haunting.

The tyres bumped against the rocky terrain as we left the forest path behind us and approached the smoother gravel leading to the main road. As the trees thinned, I noticed a strange lightness in my chest. My head cleared. A little less foggy. A little more of myself.

Was it altitude? No, we weren't that high up. Still, I had felt off all morning.

Before I could finish the thought:

"Stop!" Amelia shouted.

I slammed on the brakes.

The car jolted violently, the back wheels slipping slightly on the damp earth. Both of us were flung forward in our seats, saved only by our belts.

We sat frozen in the moment, both wide-eyed and breathless.

114

I blinked hard. "What was that? What happened?"

"I…I saw something in the road," Amelia stammered, already unbuckling her seatbelt. "An animal. Or something. It ran out."

She pushed open the door and stepped out, scanning the road ahead.

I followed, leaving the engine running, the low idle rumble oddly comforting.

"Can you see anything?" I called, rounding the front of the car.

"No, not yet." Amelia crouched down, eyes scanning the front grille for signs of a hit. "I don't think we hit it."

But I wasn't listening anymore. Something near the treeline had caught my attention. A shadow. Small and still.

I narrowed my eyes, focusing. There, just at the forest's edge. A shape low to the ground. Cautiously, I stepped toward it. The shape didn't move. It was small, maybe the size of a rabbit. That's all. *Just a rabbit*, I tried to tell myself. Yet something felt off. Wrong. Another step. Closer. Still, it didn't move. Is it dead? Another step. Now I was close enough to see it more clearly. It definitely was a rabbit.

But…

It turned its head. Slowly. Its dark, glassy eyes locked onto mine. The smell of damp mould with a metallic tang flew around me. I froze. My skin went cold, a chill crawling up my spine like spider's legs. The rabbit didn't blink. Didn't move. Its ears didn't twitch; its white fur didn't move in the breeze. It stared at me. Directly at me. It's seen me.

Then, its mouth began to curl. Into a smile. Can animals… do that? Well, this one could. I stumbled back. No. No, rabbits don't smile.

The corners of its mouth pulled unnaturally high. Not in the way of a cute cartoon bunny, but something sinister. Something too human.

There was no breeze. No birds. No sound at all. Even the usual hum of the engine seemed swallowed by the silence. The rabbit's eyes didn't shimmer with fear, they shimmered with recognition. Like it knew me. Like it was waiting. Its expression was all wrong. Its eyes too knowing. The quiet pressed against my eardrums like cotton. My name rose in my mind as if it had been whispered — *Lucas.* Just once. And then it was gone.

No, no one had said anything. Right?

It's seen me.

I didn't know why these three words struck me so deeply, but they made the hairs on my arms stand on end.

I wasn't sure how long I had stood there. Ten seconds? A minute? The shadows seemed to grow longer. The edges of my vision blurred, as if something was pressing in. Like the trees were leaning closer. As reality came back into the forefront of my mind, I shook myself from my frozen state. Without another thought, I turned and ran.

I sprinted at full speed back to the car. Amelia had just stood up when I reached her.

"What's going on?" she asked, alarmed by the look of panic etched across my face.

I gulped air. "The… the rabbit… it *smiled.*"

Amelia stared at me with a blank expression. "What?"

"In the forest. The rabbit. It was just… wrong. Its mouth-" I shook my head, still breathless. "It looked at me. It smiled."

116

Amelia blinked again, trying to piece together what I was saying. "Lucas, rabbits can't smile."

"Well, I'm telling you - *this one can*," I snapped.

Her eyes flashed with hurt at my tone towards her, but she raised a hand gently. Not to dismiss me, but to soothe. "Maybe it was injured. Sometimes when animals get hit, their mouths do weird things. It could've been disfigured, poor thing."

I didn't answer. I kept glancing back at the trees. Nothing. Whatever it was, it was gone.

"Yeah…" I muttered. "Maybe." But I didn't believe it.

We both got back into the car, both shaken. I pulled back onto the road in silence. Neither of us spoke for a few minutes. At least now the silence wasn't about *us*. It was about the rabbit. And the unease it left behind.

I glanced at Amelia just to check her expression. She was silent. Still staring at the road. What if she saw something back there too... and just wasn't saying anything? I couldn't place my finger on why that rabbit scared me so much, but it made my heart sink to the pit of my stomach. I didn't feel safe here anymore. And more importantly, I knew Amelia wasn't. I should get her out of here.

I remembered reading about uncanny animals in the forests of America. Wendigos, the article had called them. But that was Native American folklore; this was the Scottish countryside. They took forms you'd recognise but always got something just slightly wrong. A way to get close without being noticed. At the time, I'd laughed. Now? Not so much. But there was no scientific way that they could be real. Spirits, witches, possessions — whatever they were. But then what was wrong with that rabbit?

Out of the corner of my eye, I caught a flicker of movement in the treeline. Not the rabbit. Larger. A blur. Gone before I could register it. Just a shadow. Or a trick of the light. But it made my foot ease off the gas for a second too long. I took a deep breath. What was going on with me? I had never felt this on edge before.

Eventually, Amelia broke the quiet. "What are we going to say?"

I blinked, trying to pull my thoughts together. "About the rabbit?"

"No. About *Anderson*," she said firmly. "Why would we tell the police about a rabbit?"

"Oh, right. Yeah," I said, trying to blink away the image of the rabbit's smile from my mind. "We'll explain the emails, the empty cabin, the blood… the fact we haven't seen him since we arrived."

I tried to compose myself, voice still trembling. "We'll tell them everything we know."

"Are you going to talk? Or should I?" she asked.

"I will. I've got it. I just need you there to back it up, to show them the emails. I'll explain everything."

She nodded, clearly relieved. "Okay. Thank you."

We drove the last stretch in silence. I couldn't help thinking about Anderson. If he were alone out somewhere in that forest, could he survive the weather, the lack of food and water, the loneliness? And if he wasn't out there alone in the woods, then where was he? Maybe he wasn't alone.

The road narrowed as if it didn't want to let us out. Trees leaned in, claw-like branches casting shadows that didn't match the sun. I blinked, unsure whether the road was bending unnaturally, or if my nerves were just shot.

The town was small, and the police station even smaller, more like a repurposed shopfront than a government building. We parked in the gravel lot out front. I unbuckled my seatbelt and sat for a moment, just breathing. Amelia didn't move. She stared out the window, lips trembling, eyes glassy with tears she refused to let fall.

I reached out and rested a hand gently on her knee.

She flinched, startled out of her thoughts, then looked at me.

"It's going to be okay," I whispered. "We'll tell them everything. Then we can go back to the cabin, just in case he returns. We'll wait for him."

She sniffed, nodded, and smiled weakly. "Maybe we could stay in a hotel instead? Just for the night. The cabin… It's a lot."

I considered it. She was right. The place was unnerving. But if Anderson came back, we had to be there. Or at least, I did. I also felt something tugging at me, drawing me back to the forest. Maybe for the rabbit. Maybe for answers. Maybe for something else entirely.

"We should go back to the cabin," I said at last. "Just in case."

Amelia's eyes flickered with disappointment, but she quickly masked it with a tight-lipped smile. "Okay. Yeah. I understand."

We stepped out of the car.

The small-town police station loomed ahead, humble and unassuming.

It was quiet. There were only two other cars parked in the lot, and I imagined that they belonged to staff. A thick, grey blanket of cloud loomed overhead, covering the sun, hiding its view of us. The wind picked up and bit at my ankles as I slammed the car door. The weather changes so quickly out here.

We both walked toward the station door, gravel crunching beneath our weight. The sound of our footsteps and the rising pressure of the wind made it feel oddly eerie. I had never been nervous around police or anyone of authority before, but now my palms had started to sweat. There was something off about this place, not like it was haunted, but like it had seen something it had never quite recovered from. I had to wonder how many heinous crimes a small town like this would ever see in its lifetime.

There was a wall of missing-pet flyers to the left of the door. A tabby cat named Lucky. Below it, another. A missing parrot. Then a retriever. And another cat. All gone in the last three weeks. Lucas stopped counting at ten. Every single one listed a missing animal within at least the last month. To the right of the door, missing person posters. All dated this year. Five missing person posters. How could a town so small have so many missing people this year?

I followed Amelia through the station doors, but my mind stayed behind—back in the forest, at the edge of something I still couldn't name. Even inside, the scent of the forest clung to me like it wouldn't let me go.

Chapter 12

Amelia

I was waiting beside Lucas on the hard plastic chairs in the waiting area. We had sat in silence for about ten minutes now, waiting for an officer. The bright lights buzzed above us and cast a sterile glow over the grey linoleum floor. I tapped my foot, a nervous rhythm that echoed louder than it should have in the quiet.

Lucas had told the receptionist it was a missing persons case when we arrived. An *urgent* one. So why weren't we being seen? Were they not taking this seriously?

Every passing minute made me more agitated. My chest tightened with worry.

What if we've made a mistake? What if they brush this off as paranoia?

Anderson is missing; that's a fact. They *have* to help. They will find him. My thoughts circled back to the missing animal and person posters at the front door. Were they out looking for all of them every day, or had they given up already? I couldn't get my mind to settle; it raced with possibilities.

I glanced over at Lucas, who was flicking his thumb rhythmically against the zip of his jacket.

Another five minutes passed.

With a surge of nervous adrenaline, I stood up and walked over to the reception desk. Lucas followed, uncertain but loyal. I tapped my fingers against the chipped plastic counter.

My heart thundered but I wanted this over with. I needed to get everything out to another person, no longer able to keep in my worries. To either confirm there was something to be really worried about, or that we were overreacting. And I knew we couldn't have been overreacting.

The clerk didn't look up. His eyes scanned his screen lazily, as if he had all the time in the world.

Finally, he spoke.

"How can I help?" he asked in a tone devoid of warmth.

"We've been waiting a while now to report someone missing. How much longer is this going to be?" I asked, my fingers now tapping faster with nerves.

He didn't answer immediately. Instead, he scrolled through his computer again, either searching for information or pretending to.

"P.C. Jackson will be with you shortly."

"Shortly? How long is *shortly?*" I snapped before I could stop myself.

Lucas gently took my elbow and guided me back to our seats as I heard the clerk scoff behind me.

124

I shrugged my arm away from him needing space, feeling like the world was closing in, claustrophobic in the space.

"Mils, it's a police station. They're probably just busy," he murmured, trying to soothe me.

But when I glanced through the smudged glass separating us from the officer lounge, I saw two officers sitting in the break room, feet kicked up, deep in conversation.

"Yeah, they look it," I muttered.

Eventually, an aged man creaked open the door. He had to be in his sixties, with grey hair trimmed neatly around his ears, a white moustache sitting above a wide, warm smile. He looked kind. Safe.

I exhaled slowly. *Good first impression.*

"Lucas and Amelia?" he asked, already stepping aside to let us in.

We followed him into a small room that smelled faintly of old paper and harsh cleaning spray. The smell made my stomach turn. Everything felt clinical and cold, the blue-white overhead lighting burned into my eyes. The buzz from the fluorescent lights felt almost painful, growing louder in my ears and droning out all my internal thoughts. I could focus only on the low buzz. I sat next to Lucas at the metal table. The officer, Jackson, sat opposite us.

My heart wasn't just pounding anymore; it felt like it was climbing up my throat, rattling the base of my skull. My palms prickled. I felt I might vomit if I sat still a moment longer.

"My name is P.C Henry Jackson," he said, flipping over his notebook and shuffling his chair closer to the desk.

"So, tell me what's going on," he said, uncapping a pen.

Lucas launched into the story. I tried to focus, but my vision blurred. My chest felt tight again, my thoughts far away from the room.

Am I dizzy? Cold? Why do I feel like I'm shrinking inside myself?

The clock above Jackson's head on the wall ticked too loudly, each second punching into my eardrums. My hands curled into fists in my lap, pressing my nails into my palms just to anchor myself. The metal chair was too cold, grounding me when my mind wanted to float away.

"Amelia?"

Lucas's voice sliced through the fog in my head.

"I'm sorry, what?"

"The emails," Lucas said gently, pointing towards my bag.

"Right. Yes. Of course." I fumbled in my bag and pulled out my laptop, opening my inbox and showing Jackson the thread.

The older man leaned in, adjusting his glasses as he read. His brows furrowed.

"Yes… yes I see," he muttered. "And you haven't heard from him since *this* email?"

"No. And we came all this way. And the door was left open. And the blood-" my voice cracked as it all threatened to overwhelm me again.

"Yes, I understand," Jackson said, his voice softening. "We're going to do everything in our power to find your professor."

I wiped my palm discreetly against my jeans.

"With this sort of mental health worry… we're going to file this now," he added.

Relief came in the smallest of doses, enough for me to nod.

Jackson stood. "You kids go and stay at one of the hotels in the village. If you hear anything, you call me directly." He slid a small contact card across the table.

Lucas picked it up, his fingers brushing mine.

A sliver of happiness floated through me at the sound of a hotel, and the fact of not having to go back into that forest.

"Actually, Sir, I think we will go back to the cabin. Just in case he comes back, you know?" Lucas replied.

That happiness was short-lived. My heart sank. I didn't want to go back there, not after last night.

"But," I said, before stopping myself. Jackson was already showing us out the door, a gust of wind blowing in loose leaves as he opened it.

I couldn't explain to Lucas why I didn't want to go back there, not in front of Jackson. Not about the tapping at the window last night or the gut feeling something wasn't right up there. He would think I were mad.

Jackson raised an eyebrow, glancing up at the thick grey cloud that had started to come in overhead.

"I think it's safer for you kids to go stay in one of these hotels…" Jackson started, before getting caught in Lucas's unfaltering stare. Their eyes locked on each other before Jackson shook his head in defeat. "But if you insist on going back up to the cabin I'd leave quickly, the heavens look like they're about to open."

I smiled politely and offered a small nod before turning to walk back towards the car.

"You have my card," Jackson called after us. "And please, keep the doors locked!"

We both stopped and turned towards him. The wind had picked up a lot, and my hair was blowing in a frenzy. I tried to tame it, tucking it behind my ears as shivers travelled down my spine at Jacksons remark.

"But what if Anderson comes back? There isn't anyone else around, I'm sure it'll be fine." I called back, my tone matter of fact but I don't think I even believed myself.

"Yes, yes…" Jackson started, hesitantly. "I'm sure you're right. Just… be safe."

His eyes met mine and something flashed in them—kindness and worry, almost as if he were pleading. A sickening feeling settled in my stomach. Did he know something we didn't? I stood there frozen as dread crept its way up to my chest. A faint ringing began in my ears. For just a second, Jackson's small smile faltered. A flicker of something I couldn't name crossed his face. Fear, maybe. He quickly tucked it away behind his professional mask.

"And what will you do whilst we're waiting up there?" Lucas called abruptly, causing us to break our eye contact. He was clearly annoyed about being told what to do but this tone was very unlike Lucas. Jackson stood, studying Lucas.

"My job," he said, before tucking the notebook into his chest pocket and walking back into the small building.

Lucas took hold of my elbow and lead me back to the car. I couldn't help a glace back towards the police station, towards Jackson watching us from the stations window.

The car ride back was quiet. I watched the trees blur past the window, the sun now higher in the sky, making the road shimmer.

We passed a stretch of trees where the trunks grew too close together, so close they seemed to strangle each other. A crow launched itself from a low branch. I noticed another one in the trees a few seconds later. I pressed myself tighter into the seat, my throat dry, at the sickening thought that they were watching us, following.

"Do you think they'll actually look for him?" I asked, finally breaking the silence.

Lucas hesitated. "I think they'll do what they can with what they've got. Maybe as time goes on, they'll escalate it."

"And if he's not back by the time we have to leave?"

"We'll deal with that when it comes," he said. "There's no point spiralling right now."

I wanted to argue, but he was right. Still, the thought of going back to the cabin sent goosebumps skittering down my arms.

The image of the open door. The blood. The shadow.

My mind was playing tricks on me. This was a stressful situation coupled with uncertainty about my and Lucas's relationship and an unknown environment.

I couldn't help reliving last night in my mind. Not the kiss, although I wished that was what I was reliving. No. The tapping, the shadow. Was it just wind against an old cabin, the trees moving from the wind blocking the moonlight last night? Was any of it actually real? I knew one thing -- the fear I felt, that was real.

Lucas slowed as we drew closer to the cabin, his eyes darting around the view out the windscreen. I wondered if he was nervous that he would hit another animal or see the rabbit again. Perhaps deep down he didn't want to go back to the cabin either.

As we pulled up, the cabin looked the same. Still. Too still.

Looking up at it caused the lump in my throat to grow bigger. Tears pooled in my eyes. I wanted to tell Lucas to turn around. I wanted to go home, to forget that this had ever happened. Go back to normal. But I couldn't do that to Anderson, he was still out here somewhere. He had to be.

We parked beside the patch of tulips, which swayed in the breeze. I stepped out and immediately flinched, feeling a sting on my leg.

"Ow! What was that?"

Lucas rushed around the car.

"I think it was nettles," I said, brushing at my skin and spotting the patch nearby.

"Careful," he said gently, rubbing my back. "There's a lot of dangerous things out there."

"Like bears and wolves?" I joked weakly.

"Exactly," he said with a slight smirk that didn't quite reach his eyes.

But the way he looked at the treeline as he said it made me wonder if he was half serious.

I kicked off my shoes and collapsed onto the sofa. Lucas joined me after locking the door.

Silence.

130

The same awkward quiet as earlier. The air in the room felt thick with the weight of what wasn't being said.

The cabin felt different now, like I had just unlocked a door I could never lock again. The damp air still lingered inside, stale and old. The walls of the cabin creaked louder than they should have with the wind hurling around it.

"I don't know what to do," I admitted.

Lucas looked at me. "We wait. Keep busy. Try not to lose our heads."

But my head was already spiralling. What if we'd left something out and the police dismissed it? What if we were waiting here for something else entirely, something we didn't even know about yet?

"I need to move," I said, standing.

I wasn't sure what I wanted to do, but sitting stagnantly inside the cabin would not help me. I needed to clear my head. I turned my gaze towards the window, watching the leaves shiver in the breeze. I didn't want to go out there, but I didn't know what else to do. If I stuck to the perimeter around the cabin, I wouldn't get lost in the woods. And it's daytime, nothing bad happens in the woods in daylight, right?

"I think I'm going to go for a walk. Just to clear my head," I told him as I turned towards the door. My words were strong, but my trembling hands betrayed me.

"You sure?" Lucas asked, his voice was flat, but a hint of uncertainty rose at the end.

I nodded. "Just around the clearing. I'll be back in ten."
Lucas watched me go.

"Wait up! I'll come with you. I don't think either of us should be alone right now," he said calmly, but his eyes told a different story.

I laced up my boots and threw on my hoodie. My feet halted by the door like anchors. I hovered there, my hand on the doorknob, wondering if stepping outside was courage or stupidity. Lucas's words circled in the forefront of my mind: 'We shouldn't be alone right now'.

Deep down, I had a feeling we weren't alone.

Chapter 13

Lucas

I had agreed to go with her before I even knew the meaning the words. The silence in the cabin had been suffocating. I understood why she wanted to go, why she needed to. I needed to move too. But her trembling hands told a different story.

Amelia looked up at me as she opened the cabin door. "Sure, I'll meet you outside," she said, her tone uncertain. She clearly wasn't expecting me to suggest walking with her. Not after last night. Not after the forest. But that's exactly why I couldn't let her go out there alone.

Something inside me stirred, itchy and electric. The air in the cabin felt stale. Shoving myself up from the sofa, I tugged on my boots and hoodie. I didn't even know where we were going, not really. I just knew I needed to move.

My muscles welcomed the stretch. I'd always been like this: gym, running, climbing. Anything to quiet the static in my head. But this wasn't just restlessness. It was something else. A pull. A whisper.

Amelia was waiting on the porch when I stepped out the door. The cool air rushed in, sharp against my face. She leaned against the wooden railing, staring at the forest ahead. My chest squeezed with anticipation. I just needed her to hurry up. I wanted to go now. I didn't know where this urgency came from, but there was no time to stand around staring into the treeline. My foot tapped against the doorframe, fast and impatient.

"Everything okay?" she asked, her voice soft and careful. Too careful.

I didn't look at her. "Yeah, why wouldn't it be?" The words came out clipped, colder than I intended, but I didn't take them back.

She didn't push, just let out a deep breath and walked towards the door, locking it behind us.

By the time she locked it, I was already halfway to the treeline.

The forest greeted me like an old friend. The air hit differently here, crisp, earthy, and heavy with the smell of wet leaves and pine. As I stepped deeper into the trees, the noise of the world softened. The wind whispered through the branches as if it had something to tell me.

Loose stones crunched beneath my boots. The path curved upward, half-forgotten and choked with moss, but I didn't slow down. I barely noticed the sting of rain falling. My body moved with purpose. My thoughts didn't feel like my own anymore; they were quiet and distant. All I could hear was the forest.

The trees stretched high above me, swaying and alive. Bluebells clung to the last breath of summer, trembling in the wind. Ravens cawed overhead, but the sound didn't feel eerie; it felt like music. Like I was being welcomed. Like the forest was inviting me in.

134

I didn't look back to check on Amelia. She was there somewhere. The forest blurred her away.

The rain tasted sweet and metallic on my tongue. My feet moved without permission, finding a path that didn't exist a second before.

This forest was intoxicating, so much so that I almost forgot about the sinking feeling in my stomach. The feeling that had started when I took my first step into this forest. The feeling that told me to run.

As the trees leaned in, the air thickened, smelling of pine and rot.

The light dimmed. A growl of thunder rolled in the distance, but it didn't faze me. None of it did. The forest didn't feel threatening. It felt right. Familiar. Like I belonged to it, or maybe, it belonged to me.

The wind was my guide. The forest consumed me. The wind picked up, and the rain got heavier, the clear blue sky was protected from the forest by a blanket of thick grey clouds. A rumble of thunder caused the sun to hide with the sky. A bolt of lightning ripped through the clouds above, lighting my now darkened pathway. None of this bothered me. In fact, it was strangely comforting.

The rain was viscous, and the wind was tormenting. I didn't know how long I'd walked before the trees thinned. The path widened. The rain slowed.

Then, a lake.

It appeared like a secret unfolding: vast, dark and still. The clouds broke slightly, casting a pale light over its surface. Everything about this place felt untouched. Sacred and beautiful.

The surrounding trees stood too still, like an audience holding its breath.

Even the rain seemed reluctant to fall here, the drops slowing, thickening, suspended for just a second before splattering against the mud.

My pathway was lit with a scattered array of freshly bloomed tulips, leading me from the clearing directly to the lake's bank.

Its surface didn't ripple with the rain; it pulsed. Slow and deliberate, as if it had a heartbeat of its own.

The air by the lake was colder, sharper, like stepping into a pocket of another season. The scent of wet earth was laced with something metallic. Faint, but unmistakable.

The birdsong had stopped. I hadn't noticed until now. No rustle of wings, no wind against the leaves. Just the endless, heavy drip of rain onto the surface of the lake, rhythmic as a heartbeat. I looked into the treeline to see signs of any movement, any life. A lone robin sat eyeing me from a far tree beside me. Our eyes locked, or at least they felt like they did. Its head cocked to the side, as if questioning my presence, or waiting to see my next move. My eyes focused back on the lake.

I walked towards it, boots squelching in the mud beneath me. I stepped to the edge, my boots sinking slightly in the mud.

My breath caught in my throat as I crouched down. I didn't know why, but it felt wrong to stay standing here, like towering over the water would be disrespectful. I let my knees sink into the cold mud, the earth sucking at me as though it wanted to pull me closer. Leaning forward, my breath grew shallow, eyes locked on the reflection in the water.

Somewhere in the trees, a branch snapped. I jerked my head up, heart hammering. The sound didn't come from the direction Amelia would have been coming from. It came from deeper in the woods, hidden among the shifting black trunks.

I looked back down into the water, into my reflection. My face stared back at me. Sharper, somehow. Different. Still me, but something felt just a little... *off*.

I didn't look away.

Something about the water held me there. The stillness. The silence. It felt like the lake was waiting for me to see something, to *remember* something. My hand reached forward before I could stop it, fingers hovering just above the surface.

The features on my face began to swim, only slightly, gently. They floated around the surface of my face, finding their place. But the mouth was a fraction too wide. The eyes glimmered like oil on water.

My reflection shimmered, its mouth parting slightly in a soundless word.

I leaned closer, breath fogging the glassy surface.

Somewhere beneath the surface, something moved. A hand? Fingers reaching up? Or just a trick of the water? I couldn't tell. I didn't want to know.

Even so, my hand continued to reach out, trembling, aching to touch it.

The lake wasn't just reflecting me. It was studying me back. Each breath I took stirred the surface, and each breath the reflection mirrored... just half a second too late. It wasn't my face anymore; it was like something was wearing my face. Something patient. Like my reflection didn't quite belong to me. Like something was *waiting*.

The rain thinned into a mist. My heartbeat slowed to match the drip... drip... drip of water into the lake. Time slipped sideways. I didn't know how long I'd knelt there, sinking deeper into the mud, the earth tugging at me as if it had decided to claim me.

Beneath the glassy surface, something else moved, not me. A ripple spread in a slow circle, but I hadn't shifted at all. A second face, distorted, surfaced behind my own. Smiling.

"Lucas!"

Her voice tore through me, shattering whatever strange tether had bound me to the lake. My whole body flinched, pain spiking behind my eyes. For a second, I couldn't understand the sound, couldn't place it. My reflection blurred and broke apart in the water as I staggered back. I gasped, stumbling backward so fast I slipped into the mud, hands sinking into the wet earth. The forest roared back into sound and movement around me. Birds screeching, trees whipping in the sudden wind. It was too loud, like it was waking up a storm inside me.

Instantly, I felt agitated that she had intruded on this moment. The secret moment between me and nature.

The real world came rushing back. Rain. Wind. Cold. The sting of water against my face. My hearing sharpened as if a switch had been flipped. Every branch creak, every splash, every breath. My stomach twisted violently. My knees buckled. It felt like a thousand insects were crawling under my skin as every nerve woke up screaming. My hands, pressed into the mud, trembled with a numb, foreign strength, as if they no longer belonged to me.

I blinked hard. When I looked at the lake's surface again, it was just my own drenched face staring back, pale and confused. I glanced to the treeline beside me, even the robin had gone.

Amelia was crashing through the trees, soaked and panting, eyes wide. Her cheeks were red from the wind, or maybe from running, but her expression was unmistakable.

Anger. Worry. Hurt.

I stayed on my knees, frozen. She stopped a few feet away, staring at me like I was a stranger.

"What are you doing?" she asked, voice tight with agitation.

I opened my mouth, but no words came out. What *was* I doing?

She shook her head, voice dropping to something smaller. "You left me. Alone. In a forest. You just… walked off."

Her words echoed in the air between us. I flinched.

"I-I didn't mean to…I'm…" I stuttered, but it sounded weak, even to me.

"Sorry?" she said, lifting an eyebrow. "Of course you are. You're *always* sorry."

She scrubbed rain and tears from her face with the sleeve of her coat. It made me wince.

"You left me alone," she said, and I could hear the panic under the anger, like a second heartbeat.

"I-I didn't mean —"

"I don't care," she snapped, wiping rain and tears from her cheeks with shaking fingers. "I'm cold, I'm scared, and I'm *done* standing around in this nightmare while you... you zone out like a zombie!"

I opened my mouth to argue, to explain, but nothing came out. I didn't even know what had happened to me back there. Only that I'd wanted to stay.

For a moment, we stood there in the clearing, both of us breathing hard, rain running down our faces like tears we couldn't stop.

I felt a deep anger bubbling low in my stomach; it had been such a peaceful moment before. Why had she dragged me out of it?

But underneath the anger was shame. Shame that I'd left her behind. Shame that I'd wanted to stay.

For a second, I thought about staying. Letting Amelia walk away, letting the forest keep me. But her voice, sharp and angry, anchored me back.

She crossed her arms, soaked sleeves clinging to her skin. "You know what? I don't even want to talk to you right now. It's freezing. It's pouring. This place is miserable. I want to go back."

I stood slowly. "Okay. Yeah. Let's go."

She studied me, from my mud-covered knees to the look of confusion in my eyes. Looking me up and down, without another word, she turned and began stomping back through the trees. I hesitated, glancing back at the lake. There was something… *off*. Something just out of sight, tucked around the bend near the treeline.

I jogged over. A small cylinder of metal half-buried in the mud. A torch. It looked old and weathered but it was intact. Definitely not either of ours. I turned it over in my hand and clicked the button.

Dead.

Still, I slipped it into my pocket and jogged to catch up with Amelia, chest aching like I was leaving a piece of myself behind. But I

140

didn't want her to scream at me again. As I followed her, I glanced back one last time. A ripple disturbed the centre of the lake, slow and deliberate. Like something had been watching. Like something had just slipped back beneath the surface. I didn't look back again, but I knew what was there. I knew what was watching.

Chapter 14

Amelia

I had beaten him back to the cabin. He was dragging his feet behind me like a scolded child. I swung open the door and stormed inside, heart pounding and breath shallow with frustration, slamming the door behind me. The cabin swallowed me whole. From the moment the door slammed, the silence pounced, thick and heavy, as if the house itself were holding its breath.

I was furious.

My fists clenched so tightly my nails dug half-moons into my palms. I didn't feel the sting. Only the rising, choking pressure inside my chest.

What was wrong with him? One minute he was being sweet, even romantic, and the next he was abandoning me in the middle of the forest. In the middle of a storm. It was as if he had completely forgotten I existed.

I kicked off my boots. They bounced off the wall and landed with a wet thump, spraying mud across the ornate rug. No single emotion could sit in the driver's seat of my mind. Anger. Worry. Hurt. They all fought for dominance.

I leaned against the doorway of the kitchen, arms folded tight, eyes locked on the front door.

My body shook from the anger and upset that had brewed a concoction inside of me.

The handle turned.

He walked in slowly, head bowed, like a boy returning home after breaking curfew. A draft slipped through the cabin, whispering along the floorboards. The shadows in the corners seemed thicker than they should have been, the silence swelling until it pressed against my skin. The warm light bulbs flickered once, a shudder that made the shadows stretch taller across the wooden walls.

He was coated in streaks of mud, his hoodie dripping, his boots squelching softly with each step. Without saying a word, he gently closed the door behind him and lingered there, silent.

The grandfather clock in the hallway ticked a little too slowly, or maybe it was my heart rate speeding up. I couldn't tell anymore.

We stared at each other, trapped in the charged air between us. The clock's ticking grew louder, each second a drumbeat inside my head. I thought, irrationally, that if I blinked first, whatever fragile reality was holding us here would snap.

We just looked at each other. A quiet standoff of emotion and restraint.

I would not speak first. Not this time. I needed answers. Needed him to explain himself.

As if reading my mind, Lucas took a step forward. The wooden floor creaked beneath his weight. There was something different about his eyes. They gleamed too brightly. Unsettling. Not like the Lucas I knew.

"I don't know what's wrong with me, Mils," he whispered, his voice beginning to crack. "I… I lost control."

My instinct was to soften, check on him, and comfort him. But the anger had entered every part of my body, and it was relentless. I had braced myself for a fight, but what I got was vulnerability. Sadness and fear.

I didn't know how to react. How could I scream at him when there were tears welling up in his eyes?

I stood battling my thoughts for a few more moments before finally relinquishing, allowing my empathy to take the lead, but not completely dissolving the anger.

I walked toward him, pulling him into a hug. I felt his chest rise and fall erratically. A single teardrop hit my cheek. My anger being overpowered by the urge to protect him, to comfort him.

"I will never abandon you like that again. I can't believe I did that. I don't know what came over me."

"You didn't even turn around," I whispered. " You just kept walking. Even after what happened last night. Even after the fact you knew I didn't want to come back here. I called for you…"

"I didn't hear you." His voice quickened as he tried to explain. "It was like… like I was in a trance. I didn't even realise you were behind me until I was at the lake and…"

I pulled back. "Wait — lake? What are you talking about?"

He froze. His mouth parted, but no words came. He looked out the window into the trees, then back at me again.

"I was at a lake," he repeated. "It was beautiful. Massive. Quiet. You called me, and I snapped out of it."

My brows furrowed. "Lucas… I didn't see a lake."

He blinked at me. His eyes were too wide; the pupils dilated like he'd stepped from a dark room into sunlight.

"Maybe you couldn't see it from where you were standing in the trees?" He offered weakly, eyes darting away.

"Yeah, maybe," I said, though neither of us sounded convinced.

His arms wrapped around me stiffly, not with the familiar warmth I knew, but with something mechanical. As if he was mimicking comfort, not feeling it.

As we stood wrapped around each other, a quiet nagging thought floated in the back of my mind:

If the lake was really there, how could I have missed it?

I sat at the dining table with my laptop open in front of me, the screen casting a faint glow against the darkening room. Lucas sat nearby, cocooned in a blanket, hair damp from the shower. We had been sitting here for about an hour now, and he hadn't moved. He stared out the window with the same dazed expression he'd worn earlier.

I glanced at the map again. Nothing.

There was no lake.

My gaze flicked towards Lucas. He pulled the blanket up to his chin, clutching a coffee mug tight to his chest. His eyes weren't just distant; they were haunted. I recognised that look. I'd seen it before, in photos of his mum. When he spoke about the lake and the rabbit, he sounded like her, too. His fingers tapped a silent, twitchy rhythm against his coffee mug, over and over, a pattern I didn't recognise.

I turned the laptop slightly, angling it so he wouldn't see what I was typing. My heartbeat thudded in my throat. The laptop screen's glow made my vision pulse at the edges, like a migraine swelling behind my eyes.

Symptoms of psychosis.

I held my breath as the search engine was hunting for my answer. The page loaded, listing signs that appeared like a checklist of Lucas's behaviour: hallucinations, delusions, distorted perception of reality.

My stomach sank.

Could it really run in families? I had read that once. Genetic predisposition. Trauma as a trigger.

It all fit. Too well.

Believing someone is plotting against you. Believing that the TV or radio is trying to send you a message. Hearing things. This all sounded too similar to what had happened to Lucas's mum.

With everything he had been through, I could understand it manifesting earlier than it had in her. But also, if this were true and this was happening, this didn't explain Anderson.

Anderson's erratic emails, him going missing.

I closed the tab and rubbed my temples. Thinking about all of this was really making my head hurt. Lucas wasn't going crazy; I knew that. At least, I hoped that anyway. But what he said he saw, I hadn't seen that. Could it have been real?

I glanced over at him again. Still unmoving.

Still staring.

I decided to drop Charlotte another message. I wanted to know if she had reported her brother's disappearance to the police, and if she had, what had they said?

I dug my phone out of my pocket, drafted a message, and sent it. An unopened message from Charlie caught my attention, I clicked on it. A cute picture of my rabbit curled up on the small sofa with her whilst she read her fantasy novel. I smiled, hearting the photo. In that small moment, I felt like everything was back to normal. My bunny, my friend, my university. Until I looked up and grounded myself to the old wooden cabin. I sighed, putting my phone back into my pocket. I got up to fetch a glass of water. My head was throbbing; my stomach was twisted with nausea. I swallowed the feeling down and flicked on the tap. The pipes clunked as water sputtered into the glass. I had brought no painkillers with me, and I regretted that more than coming out here in the first place now right now. I pressed the glass to my lips and took a sip, ice-cold down my throat, but it didn't help. The tension was coiling inside me like a spring.

When I walked back to the living room, Lucas hadn't moved. Still staring out the same window. It was getting dark now, and even the trees were in a deep slumber with the lack of wind to disturb them.

What was he looking at? What was he looking for? I touched his shoulder gently. He flinched.

"You okay?" I asked softly, worried I had startled him too much.

He nodded slowly.

"Want some water?"

Lucas looked down at his untouched coffee in his hands. "No, I'm okay, thank you," he mumbled, eyes darting back to something I couldn't see.

I sat beside him again, unsure of what to say. I thought about bringing up my thoughts on what was going on but decided against it. I decided that bringing up his declining state of mental health and his mum would not bring any help to the situation. Right now, I didn't know how he would react if I brought up such a subject. I didn't trust the response I would get.

I closed my eyes and leaned back on the sofa, letting my mind wander. My thoughts were murky. The blog. Anderson's emails. The lake. The rabbit.

All the threads in a tapestry I couldn't piece together.

I searched for lakes in the area we were in, but nothing seemed to match my search. Now I thought about it, Anderson had spoken about a lake too. I was confused; I hadn't seen a lake. Not where Lucas said he had seen it, anyway.

Could Lucas have imagined the lake after reading about it in the emails? Or... was I the one losing touch?

I blinked away the pain in my temples. My eyes burned from the screen. My throat tightened. I was nauseous; this time I couldn't swallow the feeling down.

No, I needed air.

My throat tightened, and my skin ran ice-cold. I rushed to the bathroom. Sweat prickled across my forehead. The walls of the cabin seemed to warp around me, my vision narrowing to a tunnel.

I knew what was coming. I'd had this before. Only once. But when my anxiety got bad, it made me physically ill. I tried to brace myself for what I knew was coming, but the nausea came too fast for me to stop it. I barely made it to the bathroom before a bitter taste rose in my mouth, and my hands shook as I gripped the edge of the basin. My stomach emptied its contents into the toilet bowl. I collapsed next to it, chest heaving. The floor was cold beneath my knees. My head was dizzy. My knees slipped against the cold tiles, my body sagging under its own weight. Another wave of nausea surged through me, leaving me gasping and trembling. For a moment, I thought I might faint, that I might vanish into the blackness pooling at the edges of my vision. I sat there for a moment in the darkness.

I hadn't even turned the lights on.

I took a deep breath and steadied myself on the edge of the sink to pull myself up. A shadow moved in the doorway.

"Are you okay?" Lucas's voice cut through the dark.

I let out a breath. "Jesus, Lucas… You scared me."

He stepped into the bathroom, a silhouette in the dim hallway light. "Scared of the dark now, are we?" he joked, though his voice was oddly flat. His mouth twitched in what might have been a smile, but his eyes stayed dull and blank, the expression never reaching them.

"No, I just… this is all too much," I whispered, rubbing my temples.

Beyond the bathroom window, the trees leaned closer, pressing their dark fingers against the glass.

He nodded slowly. "Maybe we should get some rest. We can start researching again in the morning."

I stood shakily, wiping my face. "Yeah. Okay."

Lucas reached for the light switch, then hesitated, fingers twitching. His voice was soft but distant. "I'll make the bed comfortable for you." His head tilted to the side just a fraction too far, like a puppet whose strings were tugged wrong.

He left me standing in the bathroom, in the darkness, my mind a whirlwind of uncertainty.

My heartbeat pulsed against my skull. My fingers tingled and went numb. Every sound was too loud, from the gurgle of pipes to the tap dripping, like the cabin itself was mocking me. I stared into the cabinet mirror, fingers gripping the edge of the sink. My reflection looked back at me, pale and tired.

For a split second, I thought there was a reflection behind me, taller and darker, the shape wrong somehow, like a smudge where a person should be.

I whipped around, heart pounding.

Nothing.

The bathroom door was open to the dark hallway. The cabin was silent.

I turned back towards the mirror and blinked my eyes back into focus.

If Lucas wasn't hallucinating, if I was the one spiralling… what did that mean for me? What if we were both losing it? What if the forest itself wasn't what it seemed?

I watched my reflection, and for a second, I could have sworn it moved when I hadn't.

I sighed and closed my eyes. Maybe I was the one losing it.

Chapter 15

Lucas

I still felt dazed. I couldn't make sense of what had happened to me out there. Had I been at the lake, or was it a result of my sudden delusions?

My mind paced the events of earlier whilst I fluffed the pillows of the small bed. It felt too real. I had seen the lake. I had seen my reflection. That much I was sure of.

My hands moved without thinking, tugging the pillows into place. Desperate, mechanical movements. If I kept moving, I wouldn't have to think. But I thought anyway. The lake. The reflection. I *saw* them. I *felt* them. I could still feel the mist of the rain on my skin. The metallic, damp smell was still noticeable. That was real. Wasn't it?

I gripped the edge of the mattress until my knuckles turned white.

Real. It was real.

But what if it wasn't and it was a trick of my mind?

The same thing that happened to my mum.

I squeezed my eyes shut tight until I could see shapes dance behind my eyelids. No, I wasn't like her. I would never be.

I propped the pillows in place and threw the covers over the bed neatly. My thoughts were still fighting over what was reality and what was fiction. Forcing my mind to think of something else, anything else, I sat on the bed and thought about Amelia.

I wasn't sure if she would want to share a bed again after last night, but I hoped she would. I knew it was a mistake, a kiss that wouldn't happen again, but God, I needed comfort. I needed to feel something normal.

I crossed to the window and checked the latches. Locked. The flashback from the night before still sat fresh in my mind. A shiver rippled down my spine as I drew the curtains. I sat on the edge of the bed, replaying the strange moments since we'd arrived. Had I experienced anything like this before? I didn't think so.

Had I always been this way and just never noticed?

My mum used to tell me all kinds of strange things when she got sick. The texts. The calls. People standing at the edge of her garden. Eyes watching her through the window. Voices in the plumbing. Plants being dug up and rearranged when no one had touched them.

I'd believed her. For too long. Now, I recognised them for what they were, delusions. Hallucinations. Symptoms.

Is that what's happening to me now?

I went back and forth in my mind trying to secure my sanity.

I buried my face in my hands, scrubbing at my eyes as if I could erase the creeping doubt. When I looked up again, Amelia had appeared in the doorway, gripping the wooden frame like it was the only thing keeping her upright.

She gave a weary smile and staggered over.

"How are you feeling?" I asked, catching her arm and easing her down onto the bed.

She looked at me, eyes hazy, full of concern. "I'll be fine, it's just the anxiety," she said drowsily.

"How are *you* feeling?" she asked, each word filled with more concern than the last.

I hesitated. How *was* I feeling?

"I'll be fine," I echoed.

We shared a thin smile. A fragile understanding hung in the air.

"I know what happened last night isn't going to happen again. That's fine. I completely understand," I said carefully.

Amelia reached for my hand, brushed over it, then wrapped her fingers around my thumb. "It's okay. It's been tense here. I don't want to sleep alone either."

My mind spun as she crawled into bed beside me. I followed, lying beside her in a thick silence. She turned towards me and curled an arm around my waist, nuzzling into my shoulder. I pressed my hand lightly over hers, the only thing anchoring me to the moment.

We lay like that until her breath slowed and grew shallow, until her head grew heavier against my chest.

It felt like hours had passed. I stared at the ceiling, Amelia sound asleep beside me.

I couldn't sleep. My body screamed for rest, but my mind was relentless. I lay still, tuning into the wind and rain outside the cabin. Usually, I hated the English weather. The miserable drizzle and the lack of warmth. But tonight, it comforted me. It filled the silence that my thoughts left behind.

What would we do tomorrow? Go back into the forest? The thought of wandering back into that forest both excited me and sent chills to my bones all at once.

It was beautiful… wasn't it?

Then, without warning, the wind cut off.

No howl. No drizzle.

Just silence.

And then a faint scratching on the outside of the window frame.

My heart lurched. Ice in my veins. I knew the weather could be erratic up here, unpredictable, but my body didn't care. My instincts overruled logic. The stillness wasn't peaceful. It was wrong.

Deep down I knew. I knew why.

My first instinct was to sit up, go to the window and pull back the curtains, prove to myself that I was being paranoid.

I didn't move. I turned my eyes toward the window. I just… listened.

Tap, tap, tap.

No. I'm imagining it. I'm delusional. It's just a gutter, old pipes, something rational. I turned to Amelia. She hadn't stirred.

My eyes were fixed on the curtain, watching the moonlight peek through the small gaps between them. My breath sped up to keep up with my rising heart rate. My muscles froze in fear of what I knew was about to come.

Then, the moonlight was gone. Darkness spilled into the room until there was no space left to fill. Blood pounded in my ears. The room seemed to close in on me, drawing me into its darkness.

There was something outside the window.

I forced my mind back into reality, forcing my limbs to move against their will.

I was brave. I could do this. I had to protect us. Slowly, I slid her arm off me and got out of bed. My skin prickled with cold. Or fear. Or both.

You're brave. Just do it.

I crept towards the window, each step slower than the last. Every instinct in my body screamed. The air was thick with something. Whatever it was outside the window, it wanted my attention.

Tap, tap, tap.

With each bang, my muscles froze in place. I took a deep breath and reached for the curtains. The thin grey veil between me and whatever was outside.

Hairs stood at attention on my arms, my eyes wide, ready.

I held my breath. My hand trembled as it edged slowly closer towards the curtain. I stopped. I braced.

And I yanked it open.

Nothing. Nothing outside the window. Nothing, apart from my reflection staring back at me.

Full and vivid.

I exhaled slowly, shoulders relaxing. A faint ringing began in my ears. Wait, something wasn't right.

I leaned closer.

My reflection leaned too.

The glass fogged slightly, mist blooming from my reflection's mouth, but I wasn't close enough to the glass for my breath to cause fog.

Slowly, I lifted my arm. My reflection did the same.

I wiggled my fingers. My reflection did the same.

Carefully, I moved my hand towards the window.

I rubbed my finger along the condensation on the glass. Nothing changed.

The fog was still there.

It was on the other side of the window.

My heart hammered against my ribs. My stomach knotted. A cold, crawling certainty slithered up my spine.

I stared at my reflection.

A sickening feeling twisted in my stomach, it felt almost like my reflection was staring back at me. I shook my head and blinked hard, trying to rid the sinking feeling, but I couldn't. Because it *was* staring back at me.

Adjusting my eyes back, I couldn't shake that feeling.

I blinked again. *Did it blink?*

My stomach sank. *Did it blink?*

Then, my face warped.

Only slightly, slowly. But it warped.

Its eyes widened. Emotionless. Unnatural. Inhuman.

158

Its mouth contorted into a grotesque, vapid smile. Too wide. Too thin.

It leaned forward.

The reflection's pupils dilated slowly, swallowing the colour of its irises.

Its head crept towards the glass. Its eyes never moved off mine. The smile widened, reaching where cheeks should never stretch.

The reflection's hand lifted again, pressing its palm flat to the other side of the glass.

A slight cracking sound shivered across the surface of the window, small hairline fractures splintering their way across the corners.

Its hand gripped into a ball.

Tap, tap, tap.

I stumbled back. Panic overtook me. My foot caught on the bed frame, and I slammed into the wall.

Blackness took over.

"Lucas?...Lucas?"

The world returned slowly. Amelia's voice, distant at first, sharpened as she shook me awake.

My head pulsed. Every beat was a hammer strike to my skull.

"What happened?" she asked, sitting beside me and stroking my hair.

"I, there, the window…" I choked. I couldn't find the words; they were jumbled up with my thoughts. I frowned, getting frustrated with myself.

"It's okay, you're probably concussed," she breathed. "Don't talk, let's get you on the sofa and a hot drink."

I leaned into her as she helped me up. The movement sent a white-hot pain through my head. I groaned, collapsing onto the sofa.

"Hold on," she said, rushing into the kitchen.

She returned a few moments later with a small mug. Steam curled from the surface.

I took a sip. "Mils, is this… hot water?"

She blushed. "I wasn't sure if caffeine was safe with a concussion… and there's nothing else."

I smirked. "You're sweet, but this is basically tea's ghost."

She dragged a chair over and sat next to me. "So, what did you see?"

I hesitated. "It was me."

She frowned. "Your reflection?"

I shook my head. "It wasn't me. It was my reflection… but it wasn't me."

She looked away, her shoulders stiffening.

I watched her bite the inside of her cheek, her arms tightening around herself.

For a moment, I hoped she might believe me. I saw it, so I knew that. I was telling her the truth. Her eyes flickered with doubt, then softened, as if she had already made up her mind.

I started stumbling, my words falling over each other in my attempt to explain this to her.

160

"It could have been a nightmare brought on from the night before," she suggested, too quickly, as if she had been rehearsing the sentence in her mind.

My stomach sank. She didn't believe me.

"But then why was I out of bed? Why did you find me on the floor?" I said, getting frustrated.

"Maybe you were sleepwalking?" she offered, her gaze darting towards the window, anywhere but to meet my eyes.

I felt a catch in my throat. This didn't make sense. None of this made sense. But she was trying to explain it away, anyway.

"Mils…" I began, but she cut me off.

She bit her lip so hard I'm surprised it wasn't bleeding. "If there had been tapping at the window, I would have heard it," she said, firmer now. Sharper.

"My falling into a wall didn't wake you. Why would *that?*" I said, frustration flaring.

She was scared; I understood that. And confused. But so was I. Why couldn't we share these feelings together? Understand what was actually going on together. But she didn't want to. Was this her giving up on me? I was losing her.

"Okay, okay," she said, breaking me away from my spiralling thoughts. "Let's talk about it later. You need rest."

She looked at me with an expression I had never seen before. Pure fear. Was she scared of this cabin? The forest?

Or was she scared of me?

Frustration consumed me, taking over the pain that was edging into my eyes. I didn't want to talk about it later; I wanted her to believe me *now*.

She grabbed my jumper to cover me, pausing when her hand brushed a shape in the pocket.

"What's this?" she asked, feeling something inside my hoodie pocket she had just covered me with.

I had forgotten.

"Oh, I found it at the… in the forest," I stopped myself before I said lake. I couldn't say *lake* again.

Amelia tugged the item out of the pocket. The small, mud-caked object I had forgotten about. How did I forget about it?

"A torch?" She muttered, frowning. She turned it over in her hands, the mud smearing across her palms.

I felt my stomach twist as she angled it towards the light to get a better look.

Her fingers hesitated as they brushed over its surface.

"It's engraved," she said, her voice threaded with something tight, dread, maybe.

I looked down at my lap.

I didn't need to see it. I already knew.

She squinted to get a better look at the words engraved, wiping the dirt away with the edge of her sleeve. Her lips moved silently as they read. Then she took a sharp inhale, like she had just been punched in the stomach.

"It's Anderson's," she whispered.

The torch slipped from her hands and fell to the floor with a crash. A sound loud enough to make us both flinch.

"Lucas…" she said, her voice small and timid. "Where exactly did you find this?"

I opened my mouth, but no words came out. I couldn't say it. I couldn't say the word: *lake*.

Chapter 16

Amelia

It was Anderson's torch; there was no doubt about that. But why was it there? Had he had an accident? But then... where was his body?

Questions swam through my mind, slipping past before I could hold on to even one long enough to answer it. If Lucas was right, and that was still a very big *if*, and there really was a lake I somehow didn't notice, could Anderson have fallen in?

My stomach dropped, palms clammy and heart thudding. The possibilities churned like storm clouds in my chest. I needed to call the police. I had to tell P.C. Jackson what I'd found. This was evidence, wasn't it?

Still holding the torch, I turned it over in my hands, fingers trailing across the engraved name. Shouldn't he have called by now? Shouldn't Jackson be checking in?

As if he could read my mind, my phone rang. I stared at the screen. Withheld number. This had to be him.

I tapped the green button, already bracing myself.

"Hello?" I said, steadying my voice.

"Hello, Amelia?" Jackson's voice was exactly as I remembered it, measured and slightly hoarse.

"Yes, it's me," I replied, my stomach tensing. Is he about to tell me they found Anderson? I wasn't ready for that. Not yet.

"It's nice to speak to you again," he continued. "How has it been up there? I wanted to give you a quick update. We're doing everything we can, but we haven't had much luck so far."

I let out a slow exhale. It wasn't the news I had hoped for, but why did I feel like I should've known that already?

"That's a shame to hear," I replied, the tension in my jaw tightening. "It's been… okay. But Lucas took a fall and hit his head."

"What? Is he alright? Does he need medical attention?" Jackson's voice shot up an octave. Clearly, this wasn't what he expected.

"He's okay, I think," I said, my eyes drifting over to Lucas, who was curled up on the sofa, his breathing shallow but steady. "Actually, I was going to call you. I think we've found something in the forest. A torch. It's engraved. I believe it's Andersons."

Silence on the line.

"I'm on my way," Jackson said, and hung up.

At least he seems proactive now, I thought, tucking my phone back in my pocket.

I'd been sitting at the coffee table for what felt like hours, my eyes never leaving Lucas's chest, watching each rise and fall like a metronome of fear. What if it stopped? The hit to his head could have been worse than either of us had thought. But how long could you sit there watching someone breathe?

My phone buzzed. I fished it out of my pocket. It was a message from Charlotte.

I clicked on the notification.

Hi Amelia,

No, I haven't reported it to the police yet. I didn't' know if that would be the right thing, I thought maybe he could want some time on his own, but I am worried now. Are you going up there? Have you seen him?

Only so many branches swayed in the wind. Only so many birds darted past the window. My thoughts circled the drain.

I wrote a quick message back to her explaining how Lucas and I were at the cabin but there was no sign of her brother here. It didn't feel good to tell her that her brother was missing and I had to blink back tears as I put my phone down on the coffee table. I tied my hair up in a messy bun. Something about the motion made me feel sharper, more focused, and let my eyes roam the cabin. Door to door. Wall to wall. Every floorboard. Every nail. The place felt less homely now, more like a holding cell.

And then I saw it. Anderson's bag. Slouched awkwardly near the front door, slightly open. My heart stuttered.

Why haven't I looked at this already?

I rose slowly, careful not to wake Lucas. He needed rest. I stepped lightly over to the bag and peeled back the aged leather flap. Glasses case. Pen. Bottle of water. And then, a diary.

A diary.

I slipped it out carefully and crept back to the table. The leather cover was worn but familiar, his name still clear despite the weathering. *Professor John Anderson.*

I placed my hand on the cover, almost like a prayer. My fingers lingered for a second longer that necessary. And then, slowly, I opened it.

The first entry was dated two months ago. My eyes narrowed as I read.

It's hard out here. I miss her so badly.

When I told the university, I needed some time away, it was true. I needed to collect my thoughts. But deep inside, I think I came for her. I needed to clear my head., I thought this would be a great reset I needed after the incident. I miss her now more than ever.

She would have loved it here. The trees, the animals, the weather. She would have wandered through the fields and forest all day, every day. She would have picked flowers -- fresh colours in the vase each morning. She loved nature. The outdoors. Life in general. She was so full of life.

She wanted to go come out to the cabin ever since I purchased it for our anniversary. I always told her I was too busy. I told her, 'Maybe next year." What I would give now for one more 'next year'. I have no greater regret than those words.

I still do not understand it. It's like I'm living in a dream I never wake from. One where she never comes back. Like I would wake up any minute kicking

168

My stomach twisted painfully, the words burning themselves into my mind, leaving me breathless. The words blurred on the page. I sat there, hunched over the diary, my cheeks wet. My fingers tightened against the worn leather cover, my knuckles whitening. The tears didn't surprise me. I didn't know how he could have been feeling, not from personal experience. But I could empathise. I had seen what Lucas had gone through. Losing someone to themselves, how can anyone survive this kind of loss?

My breath hitched. A small, broken sound as I forced myself to close the pages. It wasn't shock exactly. It was something deeper. A sorrow that sank its claws into my chest and wouldn't let go.

Loss was a complex thing. You didn't just lose a person you loved; you lost part of your own heart. A part of you that you could never retrieve. A part of yourself that had only existed because they were there. All you were left with are memories. Pictures and voices in your head, never to be experienced in real life again.

Grief wasn't a clean break. It was messy. Constant. Lingering. I tried to still my breathing, blinking hard, swallowing down the lump in my throat. I had always felt other people's pain as if it was my own. An empath, people called me. Maybe too much of one. If there were a way to bottle someone's sorrow and carry it for them, I would have offered without hesitation. Pain didn't scare me. Watching someone sit in it alone did.

I took a few deep breaths and slowly opened his diary back up. The entries were sparse, once or twice a week at most, I guessed, as I briefly flicked through the pages. There were not many, but the ones that were written were lengthy. I flicked through to the next entry. This one was significantly longer than the previous. I started reading. Instantly I could tell it would help me understand a lot more of what Anderson had gone through up here.

Chapter 17

Anderson's diary

I had dreamed for so long to be alone, in silence and peace. Up until today, when I noticed the handprint on the window. This is the last day I will ever feel alone up here.

The array of multi-coloured tulips and mauve-lavender speckled the meadow around the cabin was the first thing I noticed when I arrived. That, and the sweet, earthy aroma of damp soil and wild ginger, like maple-syrup pancakes. That memory makes me smile. I wish I could go back to that first day.

The cabin itself is beautiful, handmade with aged wood and exceptionally cozy. A bouquet of lavender and rosemary filled the air, inside and out. Light streamed in the big window in the living room, bouncing off the walls and dancing around the room. A 'hippie's haven,' as my dad would have called it. It quickly became my favourite room.

Being from the city, I'm not used to flowers, animals, or a plethora of trees and foliage stretching as far as the eye could see. I couldn't understand how anyone could grow tired of waking up with the birds singing their melodic songs. I was in awe of the wildlife— deer, rabbits, foxes, badgers. It felt like I was living in a children's fairytale.

That was until I found what I had just found.

This place was my dream. But now, staring at the meadow outside this cabin, something feels... off. The flowers sway like dancers, but there is no wind. The air smells too sweet. And the silence — that is the worst part.

Well, that, and the muddy handprint on the window of the living room.

As I tore back the curtains to let the natural light in late this afternoon, I had noticed it. It wasn't my handprint; I hadn't been out there last night, and it wasn't there before I went to bed. I thought I was out here alone.

Am I alone?

Standing outside the cabin staring at the handprint, I've tried to rationalise what I am seeing. Maybe it's just a smudge of mud caused by a mix of wind and rain? I tried to convince myself as I stared at the clear four fingers and thumb placements of the 'smudge'. I realised there wasn't much I could do about this finding, but still my blood runs cold.

I wouldn't have noticed it if the curtains had stayed shut.

Lucy used to love the natural light. First thing in the morning, as the sun came up, she would bounce around each room of the house, ripping open the curtains and opening the windows to let fresh air and light in. She believed it would improve the mindset.

I hadn't worked in natural light since she has been gone. Not until coming here. My curtains had stayed closed.

Why did I open them up here?

When I first noticed it earlier, I tried shaking myself from my thoughts. I headed back inside the cabin, grabbed my worn brown leather satchel and stuffed my notebook and a bottle of water inside. Putting my windbreaker on, I glanced at the clock above the entrance to the bedroom door, nearly five in the afternoon. I slung my satchel over my shoulder and headed out for the third time today, and the last, may I add, making sure to lock the door behind me.

I wasn't sure why I was so meticulous about locking the door behind me, being the only person for miles around.

Lucy had always made it a habit to lock all the doors. She would go mad when I forgot. Which was more often than I would like to admit. A twinge of sadness squeezes my stomach every time I think about it.

I strode up the semi-set path beneath the towering umber-brown trees. The leaves had turned from their vibrant summer greens to molten reds and yellows. I knew it wouldn't be long before they fell and were no longer there at all. I was thankful they were still clinging on today though; they shielded me from the persistent, miserable drizzle of rain.

Everything here reminds me of her. She loved the autumn. The colours, the weather, everything about it. It was her favourite time of year.

A low fog was settling, cloaking the bottom half of the trees and drifting across the underbrush and moss-ridden tree stumps. The caws of ravens drowned out the gentle tweets of songbirds as the sun dipped below the horizon. I couldn't help but think this would be a fantastic setting — either for a children's story or an '80s slasher film.

I hiked up the semi-beaten path, winding through branches and the forgotten cobwebs threading them together. Cold, misty air clung to my face as I wiped droplets of condensation from my thick grey moustache.

The air feels different out here, heavier. I can't explain it, but I am sure that it's not just in my head.

As the wind began to pick up and whirl around me, I could have sworn I could hear a faint voice. A whisper. But a voice all the same.

I'm losing it out here.

I stopped in my tracks; I had heard rustling in the bushes beside me. I turned towards the sound and fumbled to retrieve my notepad from my satchel.

Squatting, leaning in towards the sound, I wasn't sure what would emerge from the bushes this time. But there are so many amazing species out here, I was excited to find out. As I waited, the woody incense of damp bark wafted up my nostrils. The forest's tranquillity is intoxicating.

After waiting a few more moments as the rustling continued, I stood back up. The memory of the handprint on my window made all the blood drain from my face.

I knew I should get out of here.

As I stood listening to the movement in the bushes get more intense, I felt the urge to run, run as fast as I could out of the forest. Suddenly, a long black bootlace slithered out from beneath the shrubbery.

I tiptoed forward across the terrain, tracking this creature's every slick movement. I scribbled frantically, noting down every observation I could see. Its long black body to its tiny blinking eyes assured me that this was in fact some kind of slow worm and not a snake. The eyelids confirmed it. However, this was definitely not a species of slow worm I had come across before. Its body was a sleek, almost glossy, like obsidian. Almost slimy. Its body diameter was at least an inch wider than the typical slow worm. At least half a meter in length. Was it a mutation? A new species entirely?

I documented everything.

As I continued to stalk the reptile, I noticed more movement in the nearby bushes. I paused, wondering what other creatures could lurk beside me. Realising the sun had almost set, I noted I had at best twenty minutes before darkness fell.

Suddenly, as if they were answering my thoughts, three more dark figures emerged from the bushes, joining the first along the path. Worm after worm followed until I had counted twelve in total.

Twelve slow worms. All slithering together up along the pathway, as if heading toward the same destination. The way they blinked in unison made my stomach twist. I slowly followed them.

They're not supposed to be doing that.

Slow worms were not known to be pack animals, but they seemed to move together, with purpose. I pulled the small torch from my satchel and turned it on, hoping it would not startle the creatures.

They didn't even flinch at the light, nor at me following them along the undergrowth.

The trees parted to reveal a vast abyss. With the last of the daylight fading, I could barely make out the space in front of me. Soon, I would have to rely solely on my small torch.

As I attempted to look around, trying to gain my bearings, I noticed all the creatures seemed to scurry to the centre of the void, then disappear entirely. Approaching cautiously, I noticed the beams of my torch were reflecting off the surface. It wasn't an empty space or a crater at all. It was a large, murky lake.

I swept my torchlight across the surface of the water, watching the tiny ripples break the surface in front of me.

My heart rate rose.

I couldn't seem to understand it. These slow worms were reptiles, not amphibians. They couldn't swim or survive in the water, had they actually gone in? Was there a hidden hole by the lake's edge?

As I got to the bank, I knelt and scraped my fingers across the soil, it was hard and rock-like. It would have been impossible for them to bury themselves in this, especially not as quickly as they vanished.

I brushed my fingers through the dirt, questioning whether my eyes had deceived me. I glimpsed a splash in my peripheral vision.

The hairs on my arms stood on edge.

It wasn't a loud splash, like a dog diving into the pond.

No.

178

The kind of splash you would notice from a fish whose tail has clipped the top of the water to catch an insect.

But it was now nighttime. No flies or fish should be active.

My stomach dropped, and a wave of utter dread flushed over me.

I knew I should have run.

The glare of the torch blinded me as I pointed it at the lake. The incoming mist reflected the beam, rendering me almost sightless.

I stood still.

Silent.

Waiting.

For what? Well, that I didn't know. But I knew I was waiting for something.

I steadied my breath, as if whatever was lurking beneath the surface would be listening for me. I noticed the ripples in the water were starting to get larger, more erratic.

Something was underneath the surface. I was sure of it. What was it? I allowed my imagination to run wild with sea monsters and creatures of the deep.

She had always told me that I had an overactive imagination.

Almost causing myself a panic attack, I drew my mind back into reality. The ripples in the water continued and grew larger.

I held my breath.

Water erupted from the lake, a small amount, but enough to knock me off balance. I fell to my side, close to the edge.

Scrambling to my knees, I shone my torch toward the noise.

Then I saw it. Just for a second. A quick motion. Something breached; I only glimpsed it for a second. But it was enough.

But I saw something.

I couldn't believe what I was seeing. I wouldn't allow myself to believe it. My mind reeled as it tried to comprehend what I saw.

What I thought I saw.

I scrambled to my feet, secured my satchel back in place, and ran. Staggering over the rough terrain, all I could focus on was my feet.

Jumping over old rocks and loose tree branches, I just ran. The cold air now felt hot and sticky against my skin as I sprinted along the treeline. I knew the rough direction, and that was where I was heading.

Through the canopy of trees, I finally spotted the soft glow of fairy lights that rimmed the cabin's roof. Relieved, but still on edge, I continued to run towards the lights. As the leafy terrain became softer and flatter, I saw the door. Keeping up the pace, I reached into my windbreaker pocket and grasped the key.

As I slowed, I pulled the key out of my pocket. The hot, sweaty grip of my hands betrayed me as the key fell through my fingers, landing onto the wooden deck below me.

Praying to a god that I have never been acquainted with before, I dropped to the deck, searching frantically, hoping I hadn't lost my only hope of security to the gaps in the deck wood. Next to the withered doormat, I saw the key's silver glimmer. I grabbed it and shoved it into the lock. Slamming the door shut behind me, I twisted the bolt lock, twisted the key, and collapsed onto the floor. Back against the aged sofa, face towards the door.

I sat there until my heart rate had slowed. Until the sun crept through the half-drawn curtains.

I couldn't put words together in my mind. I didn't want to think about what I saw. Because if it was real, I'm not out here alone.

I write this to document my findings. I can't tell anybody. No one would believe me, or they would put me into one of those mental hospitals. But what I saw was real. That fact frightens me. As I sit here at the coffee table writing this out, I'm haunted by the muddy handprint that remains on my window. Only time will tell how this will pan out.

Maybe I'll try to find the lake in daylight tomorrow.

Chapter 18

Amelia

My head was in a daze. I couldn't believe what I had just read. Everything he was writing was all so similar to what Lucas had said.

The lake swirled around my mind like a storm. I couldn't think of anything else.

Why hadn't I seen the lake? If two separate people were describing the same landscape, then surely, I'm the one who's going mad?

Unless…

Unless Lucas had already read this diary.

I couldn't rule out anything right now, but if he had, then why would he keep that from me?

None of this made sense. I tried to focus and read his next entry, but my eyes couldn't focus on the words. The world was spinning around me, my heart beating a million miles an hour.

I slipped the diary back into the bag, eyeing Lucas as I did so. Quietly, I did the bag back up and slid it behind the cabinet by the window. I didn't want Lucas to find it, because if he hadn't already read it, then this would only confirm one thing to him. That he was right, and I'm going insane.

I slumped back into the chair by the coffee table, trying to regulate my breath.

Frantically looking around the room for five things I could see, hear, smell, and…

Lucas stirred on the sofa, groaning as he rolled onto his side, pulling the blanket over his eyes.

I held my breath. Nothing felt normal anymore; nothing seemed right. Could I trust anyone?

I didn't want to be labelled insane. I'm not insane. I know I didn't see that lake.

I used to feel comfortable around Lucas, share anything with him. But now, sitting rigid in the hard wooden chair, holding my breath as he finally settled back into sleep, I knew I could tell him none of this. The cabin settled into an unnatural stillness, so deep I could hear the soft crack of the wooden walls adjusting to the cold.

A draft brushed against the back of my neck. It was faint, but sharp enough to lift the fine hairs along my skin. I froze, breath catching halfway through my chest.

The silence stretched, long and taut, until the weight of it felt like it might crush me.

And then—

Tap, Tap, Tap.

184

The sound exploded through the quiet, making me flinch so hard I jolted to my feet, blood in my temples pounding.

My heart thundered. That wasn't Lucas. Lucas was asleep.

My mind circled back to the other night. The shadow outside the curtains, the tapping on the window. But now I was alone, Lucas was in and out of a comatose state. I would have to deal with this alone.

The shadows in each corner of the room thickened, pooling like spilled ink, expanding and smothering. Every creak of the timber under the changing temperatures set my nerves on edge. It felt different in here now. The walls felt like they were closing in, breath by breath, until the air felt too thick to swallow.

My eyes closed as I held myself still. I needed to calm down. I couldn't afford a panic attack right now; I had to protect Lucas. I had to protect myself.

As I walked over to the door, my hand hovered over the doorknob.

"Who's there?" I called, my voice more stable than I felt.

"It's P.C. Jackson," came the reply.

I sighed a deep breath of relief and opened the door, breath tight in my chest, and stepped aside to let him through.

Jackson's silhouette filled the doorway. He rushed past me without a second word. Rationally, I knew I should feel relieved.

But for a moment, a shiver of doubt trickled through me. I told myself it was nothing, just nerves. Just fear.

I turned towards where Jackson had headed straight to; he had gone straight to Lucas. Jackson's uniform looked slightly damp at the edges, dark patches spreading across the shoulders. His shoes left faint prints on the floorboards, as if he'd come through more than just the drizzle.

Lucas didn't stir. He was curled up on the small sofa. He looked impossibly pale, as if the slightest touch might shatter him.

I quietly offered Jackson a coffee, which he accepted. I headed towards the kitchen to boil the kettle whilst he sat by Lucas's side, pulling the blanket down and brushing his hair from his face. I wanted to be hospitable. After all, Jackson had come here to help us, the least I could do was make small talk. But I kept my back turned to him, eyes out of the kitchen window as the kettle began its light rumble. I felt numb, like a zombie. Like all my emotions had been pulled out of my body, trampled on and drowned in that lake. That same lake that tormented my thoughts. I watched the window as the steam of the kettle fogged it at the edges, framing a few tall trees in its centre. I focused on the middle one, the one with a raven on its outer branch. The raven stared directly through the window at me. So still. Like it knew in this very moment that if it suddenly took flight, it might be all the shock I needed to collapse in a ball of nerves.

I wasn't sure I had even blinked; I just continued to stare at the raven as the sky became grey and the shadows became thicker.

The shrill whistle of the kettle made my heart skip a beat, causing my entire body to jolt and knock one of the mugs to the floor. It fell to the ground with a thud and shattered around my feet.

"Everything alright over there?" Jackson called, a little louder than a whisper.

186

I swallowed hard, blinking back the tears that had formed in my eyes. Finally, I caught my breath and shook myself out of my trance-like state.

"Yes, sorry, it's been a long day," I whispered back to him, bending over to collect the shards of porcelain. He didn't answer me, he didn't need to. Anyone who walked through that door right now would have been able to grasp that it had, in fact, been a long day for all of us. A long week, really.

I threw the mug's remains into the bin and quickly made a black coffee, one sugar, for Jackson. Carefully, I brought it over to him and placed it on the small table beside the sofa.

He smiled up at me. "Thank you," he said, not reaching for his coffee but instead tapping the floor beside him for me to take a seat. I obliged as if on autopilot.

"So, I'm assuming you haven't heard anything from Anderson?" he asked. The answer was obvious; he knew I hadn't. But his ability to start a conversation right now was one I was jealous of; I would gladly let him take the lead.

"No," I said, keeping my eyes locked on Lucas and picking at the skin around my fingernails.

I knew this would have been the perfect opportunity to tell him about the diary. To confide in someone else about what I had read would feel amazing right now. I knew I couldn't do that. Because if I did, and Jackson went into that forest and didn't find a lake, what would that mean for Lucas? And if he found the lake... what would that mean for me?

But then... what about Anderson? Maybe I was being selfish.

As if on cue, Lucas stirred. His eyes were fluttering, trying to find something to focus on.

"Grab him a glass of water, please, would you?" Jackson asked, leaning in towards Lucas, trying to diffuse his fog-like panic.

I found my feet and rushed to the kitchen to get the water. Relief tangled at the edge of my anxiety. Partly because I knew Lucas was now conscious. Partly because now, I didn't have to tell Jackson about the diary.

Chapter 19

Lucas

I stirred awake to a blur of colours and a sharp throbbing in my skull. My vision slowly cleared, revealing the figure of Jackson seated in front of me on the floor. My head was foggy with pain and confusion. I instinctively tried to sit up, but Jackson gently raised a hand.

"Don't move yet, give yourself a moment to adjust," he said calmly.

I hated being told what to do, but the dull, rhythmic ache in my head quickly convinced me to obey. I slumped back against the cushions, my body heavy and disoriented.

Jackson reached into his jacket pocket and pulled out a small box.

"Take these, they should ease the pain," he said, popping out two pills into his palm just as Amelia arrived, handing me a glass of water.

I didn't hesitate. Pain relief over pride. I swallowed the tablets in one go and exhaled slowly, leaning my head back, the lights in the cabin still stinging my vision. The constant banging of the wind against the cabin walls and the scatter of rain on the roof made my head feel like it was going to explode.

Amelia and Jackson moved behind me to sit on the coffee table, deep in conversation. I strained to hear, pulse quickening.

Please don't tell him I'm going mad. Not a police officer, please. I pleaded with Amelia in my mind.

"So, where exactly did you find this torch?" Jackson asked, I could hear him scribbling on his notepad.

"Lucas found it… up in the forest. There was a clearing in the trees," Amelia replied carefully, choosing her words with precision.

By the lake, I screamed internally. It was by the lake.

"Okay," Jackson said. "And were there any other signs of him? Footprints? Clothes?"

"Nothing obvious," she said. "Just the torch."

"I see, we'll need to return to that area to take a better look," Jackson said, his tone shifting.

I heard a rustling of a bag and imagined Jackson had bagged the torch for evidence.

A loud crack of thunder tore through the sky, followed by a violent downpour. Rain hammered against the roof, a flash of lightning briefly illuminated the room like a camera shutter. I winced. The combination of the noise and lighting was too intense. My stomach turned. I closed my eyes and took a few slow, deep breaths to try to still the nausea rising into my throat.

Amelia moved swiftly to close the curtains, blocking out the storm's flickering assault.

Jackson sighed. "I'll have to get another unit together and call the dog unit from the city. It'll probably be tomorrow when I can wrangle everyone together and get searching."

I rolled my eyes, instantly cringing at the pain of the movement. Another unit? Oh, please. You just don't want muddy boots.

Jackson stood. "I'll call you in the morning. Let you know when we're on our way."

"Thank you," Amelia said, walking him to the door.

Jackson paused, hand hovering near the doorknob. He turned back to me, his eyes unreadable.

"If anything strange happens, anything that doesn't feel right to you, don't hesitate to contact us."

I squinted through the amber glow of the cabin. "What do you mean... strange?"

Jackson hesitated. "We just... get the occasional odd report from these woods. Happens from time to time."

Jackson paused at the threshold, hand on the doorframe, his gaze lingering a second too long on me. His eyes were wide, unblinking. His face was perfectly calm, too calm, as if he were studying something behind me rather than looking at me. Then, without another word, he stepped into the storm and was swallowed by it.

Amelia closed the door, bolting it behind him. She turned slowly, eyes fixed back onto me.

I raised a brow. "Well, isn't he... interesting."

Amelia gave a nervous chuckle. "So dramatic," she echoed, her voice trailing off.

But deep in my gut I knew Jackson knew something more than he was letting on.

I sat up as the headache eased slightly.

The ticking clock hammered in my ears, each second a metallic stab.

Amelia sat by the window, scrolling her phone again and again, as if the glowing screen could protect her from the dark.

Why is she checking it so much? Who's she messaging?

Her expression had changed. She looked tired, yes, but also tense. Unsettled. She wasn't telling me something.

"Everything okay?" I asked, making her jump.

She slid her phone back into her pocket. "Yeah, I'm fine. I'm just trying to check the weather to see when this storm will stop," she said, her voice too quick, too rehearsed.

The wind rattled the walls, stronger this time, as a cold draft flew through the room, sending a shiver deep into my bones.

She crossed the room and lowered herself beside me on the sofa, pulling the blanket tighter around her.

"It's all just been… a lot. I just want to sleep."

She leaned into me. I wrapped an arm around her, but my thoughts were racing. Something wasn't right.

"I understand," I murmured, lying.

The thunder outside deepened, branches snapping in the wind. Our breaths fell into sync. Despite the noise outside, sleep crept in like a thief.

A crash of thunder tore me from my sleep.

The curtains flared white with lightning. I blinked hard, groggy, and pushed myself up slowly, rubbing my eyes. Does this place ever stop raining?

The trees outside howled and sang their usual dissonant lullaby. *The forest's song.* A creepy, atonal tune. Like lullabies sung in reverse.

I slid out from under the blanket, careful not to wake Amelia. I crept over to the window. My head throbbed, dark spots dancing in my vision.

I hesitated, fingers brushing the edge of the curtain. My heart thumped against my ribs.

A flash of cold hit me in the stomach as I recalled the night before. I thought of what I had seen the last time I had pulled back a curtain.

I couldn't let what I thought I saw last night to make me scared of *curtains.* I let out a breathy laugh to myself. Maybe I *was* going crazy.

In my half attempt to make light of the situation in my own head, I grabbed the curtains and pulled them back, quick. Like pulling off a band-aid.

Nothing. Obviously.

Just trees. Wind. Fog. Rain. The familiar chaos of the forest churned outside.

Every little sound became a threat.

The ticking of the clock became a hammer against the silence. The groan of the roof beams sounded less like settling wood and more like something breathing just overhead.

The storm was no longer outside — it was inside the walls, inside the floor, vibrating under my skin.

I tried to tell myself it was the weather, just the storm. But the dark corners of the cabin seemed to pulse, just beyond my vision.

I could feel it. Like something was watching us.

Still, I lingered.

What I *thought* I saw last night, I couldn't have seen.

I saw my reflection, yes, but in my tired state my mind must have filled in the gaps of what had happened after.

It must have.

My gaze drifted to the windowpane. I studied my reflection. Blurred. Muted. Normal.

Not like last time. That wasn't normal. That wasn't me.

I stared, waiting for something. A twitch. A shift. Nothing. The storm hissed and howled around the cabin. The glass fogged at the corners. Despite myself, I relaxed.

The music of the wind and rain was actually quite peaceful, beautiful really. It was mesmerising. It stood in a meditative state. And then, I heard it. Something different. Something new.

A voice.

Faint. Muffled. Melodic. The voice was female, and she was calling me.

I leaned in, eyes darting across the trees. The voice wove through the wind like a thread in fabric. It wasn't clear, but it was haunting. Like a lullaby sung underwater. And familiar. The sound grew louder and more intense as I listened closely. I could have sworn the voice was calling for help.

As though I was in a trance, I walked towards the door, ignoring the pain thumping through my head.

194

The voice grew louder and louder.

I reached the door and turned the handle, letting in a whirlwind of weather. I didn't wince as the icy air hit my body. I didn't even notice it.

With the door open the sound became clearer. It was a woman's voice. And she was definitely calling for help. The voice was so familiar, yet I couldn't quite place it. My chest tightened.

"Mum?" I whispered into the wind.

The voice grew louder. *Help me…*

The voice, it was clear now. Between the weather and the faint ringing in my ears, it was clear. I took a step into the blistering wind.

"Mum?" I asked again, louder.

A hand yanked me back so hard I lost my footing. Amelia slammed the door shut, locking it behind us. She pressed her back up against the door, hands trembling.

"What the hell are you doing?" she yelled, breathless and wide-eyed.

I stared at her, stunned, the world tilting slightly around me. The smell of wet leaves and damp mildew circled around me. For a moment, I wasn't standing in a cabin anymore, I was a boy again, reaching for a mother who was already gone. My breath hitched painfully in my chest. The ache of loss twisted tighter than the storm outside.

"I heard her," I breathed, my voice as fragile as the memory clinging to me.

I clutched the doorframe to steady myself, but the splinters bit into my palm.

That wasn't real. That can't have been real.

My mother's voice, so warm and gentle in my memory, echoed through my mind. But the voice outside, although it was the same tone, had been hollow and distorted. Wrong.

A trick of my mind, or something else?

My stomach sank. Was the forest doing this to me, or was it something rotting inside myself?

Every plank of the cabin seemed to creak independently now, groaning like an old ship. Rain tapped at the windows in strange, syncopated rhythms, like a hidden language we couldn't understand.

I stood frozen, my breath still heaving from the surge of adrenaline.

Her eyes softened into a reaction that hurt me more than anger. Amelia felt sorry for me. She hadn't moved. She was pressed against the door like she was afraid to even breathe. Her fingers gripped the lock tightly.

I blinked at her, confused. Why was she looking at me like that?

A sick feeling rolled through my stomach. I took a step forward instinctively to tell her it was okay, that I was okay, but the instant I shifted, I saw it.

The way her shoulders flinched.

The way her eyes darted, quick and desperate, toward the heavy lamp on the table.

She was afraid of me.

The realisation hit me harder than any blow. I staggered back a step, breathing shallow, like I'd been sucker-punched. I wanted to speak, to explain, but no words came. I'm scaring her and I don't know how to stop. The memory of the voice outside, my mother's voice, twisted inside my skull like a knife. Maybe it hadn't just called to me. Maybe it had *changed* me.

And maybe, deep down, some part of me had *wanted* it to.

The more I began recalling what had just happened, the angrier I started to feel towards Amelia. A deep, carnal anger. My hands were shaking, my heart hammering. My face grew hotter and hotter with each moment I thought about what had just happened. She had pulled me away from something so sweet, so warm, so enticing.

I caught myself as my hands began to turn into fists. I couldn't be angry at her; she was only trying to protect me. But the rage still whirled around inside. She was standing between me and what I so deeply longed for.

I watched her as the look of concern in her eyes slowly began to turn to fear.

Should she be scared of me? I didn't know.

But what I did know: I was scared of myself.

My legs gave way as I slowly started collapsing to the floor. The wood was hard and cold, like raw stone. It didn't faze me, I didn't really notice, I was trying to control all the emotions that were trying to escape. I didn't know how to feel. Dropping my head into my hands, I started to sob. Maybe because my emotions were getting the better of me. Maybe because I had hoped the tears would wash away the fact I was going insane.

Amelia stood at the doorway watching me. She didn't run over to comfort me this time.

Chapter 20

Amelia

What was happening? What was he doing? I stood there, frozen. My lips parted, but no words formed. My expression said it all — confusion, fear, disbelief. Lucas slumped against the wall opposite me, mirroring the same blend of emotions on his face. His chest heaved with each sob that escaped him.

"What is going on?" I asked softly, my voice trembling. A chill climbed my spine, not from the wind howling outside, but from something darker unravelling in front of me.

"I heard her," he repeated, eyes wide and unfocused. His voice was timid and childlike, the voice a little boy might use after breaking his mother's favourite vase.

"Who? Who did you hear?" I asked, a sharp edge of irritation cutting into my confusion. My pulse was racing now. There was a long pause. He didn't meet my eyes. I froze for a second, heart thudding painfully against my ribs. He wasn't just crying; he was unravelling.

Each sob ripped out of him, raw and broken, as if something deep inside had finally given way. His hands clawed at his hair, yanking at it, as though he could physically pull the pain out.

"I heard my mum." He said it so quietly I almost didn't hear it. But I did. Every syllable hit like a stone to the chest. He kept his gaze fixed on the floor, more tears pooling in his eyes before slipping down his cheeks. My breath caught. Something inside me cracked. Even through my anger, through the fear clawing its way up my throat, I felt the pull to comfort him. Not yet. He had to explain first. I needed to understand.

"Lucas… your mum's —"

"Dead. Yes. I know. My mum's dead," he snapped, cutting me off. His voice was blunt, but the tears didn't stop. They flowed freely now, unchecked and wild.

I felt my own cheeks dampen. I hadn't even realised I'd started to cry.

He's unravelling. That much was clear. But what could I say? What words could hold him together?

He's struggling.

I edged closer, cautiously. His breaths came in jagged gasps, the kind a body makes when it doesn't know whether to breathe or scream.

"Then… I don't understand," I whispered, voice cracking under the weight of it.

"And you think I do?!" he exploded, leaning back as though my confusion had struck him physically. I flinched. I knew about grief, I knew about the stages. Denial. Anger. Bargaining. Depression. Acceptance. Maybe he had only just reached stage two. Perhaps this forest, this storm, this isolation, had forced him to confront it finally. But it was killing him. My chest tightened so painfully I thought I might fold over with him.

He squeezed his eyes shut and rocked forward, burying his face in his hands. The entire room seemed to shrink around him, pressing in.

I could hear small sounds slipping from his throat now. Not words, just fragments of grief, broken things. And then his body jerked. A small, uncontrollable twitch, and a sound escaped him that chilled my blood: a child's whimper. God, he sounded so young in that moment. Not the Lucas I knew. I collected my thoughts. If I had to be the strong one and get him through this, then that is what I was going to do.

"I think tomorrow… once Jackson's done whatever he needs to do, we leave this place. Get a hotel. Or go home. We both need to breathe," I said cautiously. Pushing him now and demanding answers would only push him further into the dark.

I dropped to my knees beside him, hesitating for just a beat before I reached out and laid my hand carefully between his shoulder blades. He flinched at first, the muscles in his back locking tight. But I kept my hand there, firm and steady. I could feel the storm inside him. Every shudder, every stifled sob, felt like an aftershock rumbling beneath my fingertips.

Tears filled my eyes without permission. I blinked them back. I had to stay strong.

For him.

As I kept my hand on him, I hummed. Not words, just a soft vibration of sound, hoping to anchor him back to something solid, something real.

Something inside me screamed at me to get away from him; he wasn't safe. But I forced myself to stay, to soothe him. I needed to help him. I *could* help him.

Slowly, painfully, his breathing evened out.

The violent shaking softened.

"You need to sleep," I said, helping him to his feet. He was almost deadweight, heavier than I had expected. I planted my feet firmly into the ground as I used every bit of my strength to get him up. His legs were wobbly. Like Bambi on ice. I ducked underneath his arm to help bear his weight, guiding him gently to the bedroom. I untangled myself from him as he dropped onto the bed. My fingers ran softly through his hair as I sat beside him until his sobs subsided and his breathing stilled. Until he finally, mercifully, fell asleep.

I slid out of the bed and tiptoed toward the window. The fog clawed at the trees like ghosts in slow motion. What was he so captivated with out there?

I drew the curtains closed and crept into the living room, easing the creaky bedroom door shut behind me. If he tried to leave again, I'd hear him.

I curled up on the sofa. Tired, emotionally drained, I cocooned under the throw blanket.

Outside, the storm whispered and sighed, the sound almost tender now. A lullaby meant to rock me into forgetfulness. I let my eyes drift shut.

202

Tap, tap, tap.

My eyes flew open. My heart launched into my throat. I didn't move. I felt myself holding my breath. The sound was faint, but it was undeniable.

Purposeful.

The relief I'd felt a moment ago drained out of me like blood from a wound. I was stuck, every instinct in my body screaming: *Stay still. Stay quiet.*

I may have just rationalised everything that's happened with Lucas, but here alone in the dark, my blood ran cold. I could feel my heartbeat pounding in my ears.

Tap, tap, tap.

I couldn't tear my gaze from the curtains and the window they concealed. The sound was rhythmic. Purposeful. Like someone was knocking. I sat up slowly, gripping the blanket to my chest. I wanted to go over to the curtains, pull them back, prove myself right that there would be nothing there. But my legs would not move.

I squeezed the blanket tighter around my chest, feeling my nails dig into the fabric. I could hear my breath rasping shallowly in the silence between taps.

Still, I couldn't look away from the window. It was as though something on the other side was pulling my gaze toward it, coaxing me forward.

My legs felt rooted to the sofa, my muscles trembling from the strain of holding still.

I remembered Lucas's window incident, had it started like this?

Tap, tap, tap.

I had to look.

I had to prove it to myself.

With agonising slowness, I slid one leg off the sofa. Then the other. My bare feet kissed the cold floor, grounding me in its bite.

I forced myself to move, against all my instincts, each step heavier than the last. My body screamed at me to stop, but I couldn't.

Each creak of the floorboards beneath me was a gunshot in the otherwise suffocating silence. I arrived face to face with the curtain. My hand hovered over the fabric, trembling uncontrollably. The urge to run, to hide, to scream, fought viciously with the cold, rational voice in my mind. I squeezed my eyes shut, inhaled sharply, and snapped them open again.

Just do it.

One hand shot forward. I seized the curtain. Yanked it open.

Darkness. Nothing. Nothing but the pale outline of the trees swaying in the wind.

My pulse hammered against my temples so loudly it was no wonder that I couldn't hear the storm anymore.

Tap, tap, tap.

I leaned my face against the window, hands around the side of my face to block any stray light. My heart was pounding. My hands were shaking. The glass fogged with my frantic breaths. I squinted. Left. Right.

There, to the side, something moved.

I stiffened; my whole body locked in panic.

I locked my eyes on what I was seeing.

204

An old piece of guttering was dangling from the roof of the cabin. It had not survived the storm.

Tap, tap, tap.

The guttering banged against the side of the outside wall. The wind circled around the cabin, engulfing it in its chaos. I stepped back and drew the curtains closed.

I almost laughed, almost, but it came out as a ragged exhale instead. My muscles sagged with the overwhelming weight of adrenaline draining away. Of course, it was just the gutter.

But my hands were still shaking.

Still, something inside me didn't quite settle. I tried to convince myself it was over, that I'd proven the tapping harmless. But my steps felt wrong, misaligned with the world I thought I knew. Each creak of the floor seemed sharper now, every shadow deeper.

Even when I settled back on the sofa, I couldn't shake the feeling that the tapping hadn't been a mistake.

A soft creak, close, too close, came from somewhere deep within the walls.

Not the gutter. Not the storm.

Something inside.

My breath hitched in my throat. I turned my head slowly toward the hallway, where darkness pressed up against the edges of the living room like a living thing.

I strained my ears, heart hammering, telling myself it was the house settling. It had to be.

But I didn't dare move.

The tapping might have been explained. The tapping was the wind, the gutter.

But the creaking?

The creaking was inside.

And this time, I wasn't sure I could explain it away.

I settled slowly back into the sofa; eyes fixed on the dark corridor. I pulled the blanket up to just below my eyes, like a child. Like a blanket would protect me from a monster.

I tossed and turned for what felt like hours. There was no way I was going to sleep after that. Even when my brain rationalised it all and I was on the brink of drifting off, the dark looming hallway would fall to the front of my mind, and my eyes would jolt open in a panic. After countless attempts, I decided that sleep was not on the cards for me tonight. I shuffled myself upright on the sofa, letting my eyes adjust to the soft orange glow of the one living room lamp I had left on. My safety lamp.

I leant forward and grabbed Anderson's bag. Shuffling through the contents, I grabbed his diary. A bit of late-night reading never hurt anyone, I concluded. Perhaps it'll even help me drift off to sleep.

Chapter 21

Anderson's diary

I dreamt about her last night. Once I had woken, it took me a while to realise that it was all it was. A dream. I wish it hadn't been. She had been here. She had walked out the front door with me, hand in hand, into the gleaming sunlight. Leaving her favourite flower on the steps on the porch before we left, for protection. She had always said tulips evoked love and light and warded off negative energy. And she had always tried to protect us.

I wished I had never woken up.

It took me a moment to piece together where I was, what I was doing, and what on earth had happened last night.

What did I see? A thought that has circled my mind since I returned from the lake.

The weather had worsened this morning. Thick mist now coated most of the trees that surrounded the cabin, allowing only brief glimpses of yellow and maroon leaves to poke through. The rain was heavier, and from the soggy grass and sloppy mud at the forest's entrance, it seemed it had been raining all night. There were no animals in sight. They were all hiding from this miserable weather, just like I was.

Could my mind have really created the horrific sight I saw last night?

I recall reading a recent psychology study that theorised when people see unexplainable things otherworldly such as ghosts or aliens, it might actually be their minds way of protecting them, covering up something much more sinister that they have witnessed, or a trauma that they have experienced.

Could I have witnessed something so disturbing that my brain replaced it with… that? But what could be worse than what I saw last night?

If I had ever witnessed something worse, well, I never wanted to find out what that could have been.

People go crazy when they're alone.

Stir crazy, they call it. The mind can turn on itself. It plays tricks.

It's hard to understand, isn't it? That your brain, the thing that makes you "you", can deceive you?

The ultimate betrayal, really.

I considered emailing Amelia to tell her about last night. I just wanted someone else to know. Someone else to confirm I wasn't losing my mind. But I decided against going into detail. I didn't need her to think I was going mad.

I instead decided to compose a more appropriate email. It took a while for my email to send as the internet was not playing ball today. I guess it was probably because of the storm setting in.

I also considered messaging my sister. I don't really have many people to confide in these days. My better judgement kicked in, and I decided not to. I didn't need her to worry about me, and with her living so far away, I didn't want her to splurge on a flight just to come and make sure I was okay.

I tried to distract myself with research, but none of it was going in. My thoughts kept circling back to the lake. Swirling. Whispering. Tormenting.

That place was all I could think about.

I know I shouldn't go back. As soon as the storm calmed, I knew I should have packed and left. I should drive back home, go back to work and return to my studies.

I also know that it is not what I am going to do.

I cannot take my mind off the lake.

The feeling that something is waiting for me.

Something is out there. It wouldn't be very scientific of me to run away when I was this close to a breakthrough.

A breakthrough of what? I guess I will find out.

My mind was in a daze earlier today, like a living dream. The feeling of fear and confusion kept bringing me back to the dreaded night. The night I found my wife. I felt the shock, the dissociation. I had heard the whispers in the halls when I finally went back to work after the funeral, that my eccentric behaviour drove her mad. That my craziness rubbed off on her. The words hurt; they stung like needles to the heart. But were they true?

I cannot think about that now.

I went back up there this afternoon. I laced up my boots, threw on my windbreaker, and grabbed my torch. No notebook this time, I had a feeling it wouldn't be needed. Not in the rain. Not with whatever was out there.

When i opened the cabin door, my heart sank.

Right there on the porch in front of me were my dried muddy boot prints. Protected from the rain the night before. But next to them were fresh ones.

These were still wet.

Prickles of cold travelled up my spine.

The boot prints were heading toward the door, but there were none leaving.

Lightheaded and dizzy, I stumbled back. All the effort I spent convincing myself that last night was a hallucination, this shattered it. The reality of the situation slapped me in the face.

I took a moment to breathe, contemplating my next steps.

Was I still going to the lake?

Yes.

Did I want to?

Hell no.

I took a step out of the cabin door, cautiously looking both ways around the cabin, checking for any movement.

Nothing.

210

I decided I would scope out the boot prints first, hoping I would see them leave, and that whatever had been there was long gone. I veered left, circling around the side of the cabin, following the wet muddy boot prints.

They led around the cabin, right up to the window of the living room.

They faced towards the window. They stopped there.

Right to the window with the curtains half-drawn.

Right where it would have seen me sleeping on the sofa.

Whatever caused these footprints had been watching me. Where had it gone? There were no more footprints leading away.

Had it just…vanished?

A shudder of realisation flushed through my body.

No one would hear me out here. No one really knows where I am. If something happened… no one would ever know.

I turned and headed down the porch steps out into the forest. I needed to get to the lake.

I didn't know why.

I couldn't understand it.

Anyone in their right mind wouldn't go back up there after they had seen what I saw.

But I had to.

I froze when I saw what was on the bottom step. Alone in the middle of the step, placed with purpose. One small, pink tulip. My wife's favourite flower.

It was a sign. She is still here with me. My beautiful Lucy. She was always looking out for me. She still is. I bent down to pick up the flower, twisting it in my fingers. A flow of tears streamed down my face, and for the first time since I lost her, they weren't tears of sadness. But of hope.

I slipped the tulip into my bag and tried to focus on keeping my feet from slipping beneath me as I trudged into the treeline. Visibility was poor. The combination of thick fog and heavy rain made it almost impossible to know where I was going.

But I knew.

Deep down, I knew.

Something inside me kept pulling me forward, as if a rope were guiding me. Pulling me along the path.

'Stay curious, but be careful, remember?' Words Lucy would always tell me before a work trip.

I missed the way she would always worry about me.

I stepped over logs and debris. My movements, fixed and mechanical, almost trance-like.

The fog clouded around me. It engulfed me in its heavy silence. The air was so damp I almost choked on it. I took in deep, slow breaths and continued on.

Finally, I reached the opening in the trees.

It looked different here now in daylight. Even though it was still foggy, it felt a lot more welcoming. I wasn't getting wet anymore. I looked up, the rain had stopped, I hadn't noticed when. It made me glad.

Walking to the lake, I knelt, getting my hands and knees covered in mud and dirt. I leaned forward, peering into the water, looking deeper and deeper into the lake. Looking for movement, colour, anything that told me there was life of some sort here.

The water was still. Perfectly calm.

Time fell away.

I forced myself to blink. The rain had stopped, the wind now too. Everything was still.

I let out a small laugh of relief and shook my head.

It was all in my imagination.

Of course, it was.

Last night was a dream, a trick of exhaustion. This place was real. Beautiful and serene.

Maybe I was going crazy, maybe the professors were right. Maybe I was the problem.

Then I remembered the boot prints.

If it were all in my head, like I had tried to convince myself, then there wouldn't have been any boot prints.

A chill ran down my spine.

I looked back at the lake.

My heart stopped.

All the blood drained from my body.

I couldn't move. I couldn't look away. I just stared at it.

Staring at my reflection.

The same tired eyes, the same greying beard, the same short hair.

The same look of shock on my face that I could imagine I was displaying. It was me in my entirety.

Except that a reflection in a pool of water should be faint, almost blurry. This was crystal clear.

So clear, in fact, that it was almost as if I were beneath the water looking up at myself.

So clear that I could have reached out and touched the face.

The reflection stared deep into my eyes.

It was all in the eyes.

There was just something ever so slightly off about the eyes. They were too wide.

Like a worn-out animatronic.

Dead. Lifeless.

Is that really what I look like? Is that how people see me? My mind spiralled.

It just stared.

So did I, frozen in place, unable to breathe, unable to move.

Its mouth twitched a second too late. Out of beat, out of sync.

 Was my mind playing some sort of trick?

The face began to contort. Not dramatically, but like the skin was trying to remember how to fit the bones beneath.

My features trying to find their correct positions on the surface of my face.

The reflection moved closer.

Closer to the surface of the water.

Closer to me.

I jumped to my feet.

Without another look, I ran.

A splash of water erupted behind me.

I didn't look.

I just ran.

214

I knew where I was going this time.

I wasn't thinking; I just sprinted down the slippery pathway back to the cabin.

The rain had started again. Wind howled. I lost my footing, catching my balance on a nearby tree.

I could see the lights, and I picked up the pace.

Was it following me?

Was I leading it to the place I slept?

Did it already know I stayed there?

I didn't turn to look.

Grabbing the key in my pocket, I made sure I had a firm grip this time.

I shoved the key into the lock. I got in. Slammed the door. Locked it.

Double locked it.

I ran to every window. Checked the latches and pulled the curtains shut.

My heart was pounding. My head was dizzy. My breath was short.

I was safe now.

I rushed into my bedroom and locked the door too.

Pacing, trying to slow my breath.

It wasn't working.

My body trembled, mind reeling.

Like the child I used to be, I threw off my boots, crawled under the covers, and hid.

As I write this, the wind outside the cabin has stilled. I think I'm going to try to sleep through the time. I'll admit, this is the first time in a long time I have ever felt this frightened.

I think that perhaps tomorrow it'll be time to leave.

Chapter 22

Amelia

My brain could barely comprehend what I was reading. Was this some kind of sick joke? Perhaps it was a story he was drafting, something to pass the time by whilst he was out here alone. Maybe he was writing his dreams, trying to make sense of them. Those would have made much more sense to me than this being a real diary entry. And those things I would like to believe, and would believe, if I hadn't been watching Lucas go through very similar experiences. The fact that Lucas had also been terrified of something outside of this cabin, that he was also talking about a reflection, that he also seemed like he was losing his mind... those were the things that sent ice cold chills scattering over my skin, shivering down my spine and back up to my heart that palpitated with every breath.

I sat for a moment, staring out the same window Anderson would have stared out when he was here. If there was something out there, really out there, then wouldn't I see it too?

I didn't understand this place anymore, not that I really ever had. The thought of packing my bags now, leaping into the car and driving as fast as I could away from this place was the most enticing thing I had felt since my kiss with Lucas. But I couldn't. I knew I couldn't. First, Lucas definitely has a concussion, and I can't drive. Second, trying to convince Lucas to leave right now filled me with more dread than the ink in Anderson's diary. I couldn't trust how he would respond. Lastly, I couldn't give up hope of finding Anderson. He is the reason I am here, and I don't give up easily. No matter how much my body wanted to collapse to the floor in a stress-induced meltdown.

Closing the diary, I slowing slid off the sofa and tip-toed towards the kitchen. I didn't want to risk waking Lucas; my head couldn't cope with enabling more madness right now. The pipes clinked as I turned on the cold tap and splashed my face, hoping it would wake me from this insanity. Instead, it just hid the tears that silently streamed down my cheeks. My tastebuds recoiled at the metallic taste that lingered in the water, but my body drank it down in one go in a rush to ride the migraine that was now forming behind my eyes. I did not know what to do. How would someone else act in my situation? Would they run? Scream? Or quietly push down all their feelings in their chest and be strong for Lucas? I decided to try the latter. It seemed like the only logical thing to do right now, my only option. I watched as the wind whipped through the trees and blew the leaves rapidly around the cabin like a mini hurricane. Rain poured down from the dark clouds and hammered on the roof of the cabin like a white noise machine I couldn't turn off. Everything felt so loud and so quiet at the same time, it felt like my brain would pop. I wish I had brought some earplugs. I took a deep breath in, and my heart rate began to lower as I focused on the incessant hammering.

Slowly walking back into the living room, I stopped at the bedroom door and poked my head in. I saw Lucas stir slightly as he wrapped himself further into the blanket. Guilt flooded my chest as I realised how easy it would be to grab his car keys and leave right now. Take my chances at attempting to drive through this storm. I could be halfway home before he would even know I was gone. I shook the selfish thoughts from my mind and sat back in my chair, staring at the horrors that I was sure would await me inside Anderson's last diary entry. Sliding my phone from my pocket, I decided to call Charlie before I read more. I wanted to tell her everything. To gain some clarity from an outside perspective on this situation. Perhaps she would tell me I was overreacting and that everything was fine. God, I hoped she would say that. The harsh beeping from the other end of the line washed away my hopes. No connection. The storm must be interfering with the signal.

What is wrong with this place?

I let the realisation that if anything happened tonight, I couldn't even call for help, float to the back of my mind. I couldn't add that to my list of anxieties right now.

I decided at this moment the only thing I could do was rip the band-aid off. I opened Anderson's diary, flicked through past whatever craziness I had read before, and found his last entry. Swallowing down the sickness that rose in my chest, I took one final deep breath and read.

Chapter 23

Anderson's diary

I stayed under the covers long enough to be sure I must have fallen asleep at some point, but with how exhausted and dazed I still felt this morning, I was unsure if I could ever have a good night's sleep again. Unsure whether it was night or day, I decided it was time to brave getting up. Reluctantly, I pulled the covers from over my head and lay there, silent and still. It was dark. Not what I had been hoping to see.

Praying that daylight would come and save me soon, I reached to my bedside table and twisted around the alarm clock. It was two-thirty in the morning.

The cabin was quiet, eerie in its blackness. I could hear the wind rushing in a hurry around the trees, the rain pattering on the old roof. In the right circumstances, it would have been beautifully peaceful. Now, it filled me with dread.

I lay back, staring at the ceiling, my mind reeling from what I'd seen at the lake. I still couldn't comprehend it.

I couldn't quite recall the hike up there, but I remembered the terrible weather. The wet, earthy scent of the lake mixed with a hint of moss and damp tree bark. The absolute stillness of the rain and wind as I approached it. I remembered my reflection, and what it had become.

I remembered running back. Locking the windows. Locking the doors. I remembered the second set of footprints.

I don't know what was happening to me. Even for an intelligent man like me, this was tough.

I know I should never have come out into nature. As a child, my parents would only take me on city breaks. My father wouldn't allow a trip to nature. We're not hippies, so why would you want to live with the birds and animals? He would say. Maybe he was right.

Should I seek a local psychiatrist? Go for an examination tomorrow? All these questions circled in my mind.

After being alone for this long, the probability that I am losing my mind seemed higher than the possibility that my reflection had somehow turned on me.

It had all felt so real.

Was I really not able to distinguish fantasy from reality?

Trying to take action, I sat up and threw off the covers. I perched on the edge of the bed, attempting to come to terms with the idea that I was safe. That nothing could harm me here.

I am an adult.

Even as a child, I hadn't believed in monsters. Still, I got up quickly and flicked on the lights. I stood frozen. Everything went silent.

So incredibly silent.

I could have sworn I had heard the rain moments before, but now, nothing.

Maybe I had been so deep in my thoughts that I hadn't noticed it stop.

I was alone. I knew this.

And yet… something was wrong. Deeply wrong.

A slow, sinking dread settled in my chest. I felt unsteady. On edge. It was deadly silent. If a pin had dropped, I would not only have heard it, I would have run.

A wave of earthy, damp air hit my nostrils. I instantly recognised the smell.

Tap, tap, tap.

My blood ran cold. That simple noise cut through the silence like a scalpel.

My heart rate soared; I felt physically sick.

I slowly turned my head towards the window. The curtains were drawn.

Tap, tap, tap.

I tried to slow my breathing.

It's a forest, I told myself. It could be anything.

A woodpecker, tapping its beak on a nearby tree. A broken branch that had half-fallen and was scraping against the others.

An insect. An animal. The wind.

Anything.

Tap, tap, tap.

I knew deep down this was none of those things.

With every molecule of my being, I wanted to scream.

To run. To hide.

But I couldn't move.

Tap, tap, tap.

I would not face this. Not tonight. Not ever.

I forced one leg forward, slowly placing a foot on the floor.

Then the next.

Careful. Silent.

I hoped that whatever this was couldn't see my shadow beyond the curtains.

I felt tears threatening. I slowed my breathing, trying to suppress the rising panic.

Tap, tap, tap.

Step after step, I moved toward the bed.

Until I finally reached it.

As I sat down on the edge, the floorboard betrayed me with a sharp squeak.

I froze.

Held my breath.

I stood still for what felt like an eternity.

Waiting. Listening.

Nothing.

Slowly, I climbed back into bed, pulled the covers over myself and curled in, thankful the lights were still on.

Tap, tap, tap.

I guess not all monsters are attracted to the shadows.

I lay there, paralysed. My imagination tore through every corner of my mind.

I waited for the tapping to return.

For something worse.

But that was the last sound I heard all night.

The metallic scent mixed with moss and decay faded.

Eventually, the rain started again.

Then, thankfully, morning came.

I heard the birds beginning their first songs. Hours had passed. I had laid under the covers in silence the whole time. Finally, I pulled myself out of the bed and went to the curtains. After a moment of psyching myself up, I ripped them open.

Nothing.

Nothing but a very slight crack in the window's corner. Had something tried to get in? I looked closer. The crack, I imagined, should have come from outside the window, if something was trying to get in. This crack, it seemed, was inside the window.

I stared at the crack, trying to make sense of it.

I remembered Lucy always asking to come somewhere like this. A beautiful remote cabin, just the two of us. I was always too busy with work, I had told her. Maybe if I had gone somewhere like this with her, I wouldn't be at this cabin now, alone. She would be here with me. I remembered our fights about my workaholism, it was actually one of the last things we had spoken about.

I left the bedroom and walked to the kitchen. Whilst my coffee was brewing, I began searching for a local psychiatrist.

Before I could reach out to anyone for professional help, I realised that I had to talk to someone. Someone I knew. Someone I trusted. This was too much to face alone.

I opened my email and wrote to Amelia. A quick summary of my experiences.

I remembered the way she had always supported me in my eccentric ways. After my wife died, she was the only person who didn't speak behind my back. She actually left me a box of chocolates on my desk. She had empathy and was accepting. I just hoped she would be open to understanding this.

I sat for a moment after sending and drafted a second one. I typed it out, deleted, re-typed it.

I had to get this one right. The first one may have been a little too honest.

I clicked send.

Error.

The last email bounced. The storm had knocked out the internet again.

Frustrated, I tried once more.

Sent.

I smiled with relief.

I needed someone to talk to. Amelia was smart.

And the truth was, I didn't really have anyone else.

I found myself just staring at the black screen of my laptop, now falling asleep from inactivity. My reflection stared back at me.

It was a face I had seen my whole life.

But now, it felt more threatening than familiar.

I got up and made another coffee. Hoping it would shake me from my dissociative state.

I stood at the kitchen window, watching the forest sway in the wind.

It looked the same.

But it felt different now.

I can't explain it.

Even the trees seemed to move differently, twisting violently, as if they knew something I didn't.

I jumped and turned to look behind me quickly. I could have sworn I had just felt something on my shoulder. Just for a moment.

I hurried around and double-checked all the locks on the windows and doors. Then triple checked.

I was locked in. Safe. Alone.

Maybe I am losing it.

Maybe not.

All I know is that the idea of going back to the lake…terrifies me.

Every logical part of me says to stay away.

It was a forbidden fantasy. Sweet in its bitterness.

No sane person would return to that forest, to that lake.

And yet, deep down, in some hidden, unspoken part of me -

I knew I had to go back.

After about an hour of pacing from room to room, I was still waiting for Amelia's answer. She must have been asleep. I knew that, but I couldn't help but check the screen again.

Still nothing.

She believed in me. She supported me. Unlike anyone else back at the university, Amelia listened to me. She hadn't just brushed off my concerns or twisted them into questions about my well-being. She could help me.

The early morning light shone in through the curtains, blinding my line of sight as I stood. Blinking heavily, I walked over to the window and shut it. As my hands reached out for the fabric, something gnawed at the edge of my memory. Hadn't I already closed them last night?

I paused for a moment, trying to recall when I would have gotten up to open them. My mind was foggy, as if I were trying to recall a half-remembered dream.

My memories started flashing back to me in small, fragmented pieces. I remembered the tapping, the fear I felt. The shadows and figments I saw in the corner of my eyes would vanish when I tried to get a proper look.

Everything seems a lot lighter during the day. It's not just the fact that the sun was up, the air felt lighter-less oppressive. The air isn't heavy on my chest like it felt last night. I feel calmer. I can think more clearly. I feel… almost normal.

I am safe in the daylight… aren't I?

I breathed in deeply and let the coffee anchor me. I could think more clearly in sunlight. I know I'm not going to be heading outside today, but I can't get the tapping out of my mind. I wonder if there would be more footprints outside., I dare not check.

I can't get these lingering thoughts of last night out of my head. Those slow, rhythmic knocks at the window. I half expect to hear them again at any moment, echoing through the walls, bringing the unease with them.

I won't look outside.

I think I need some sleep. I think I got next to none last night. Maybe after a short nap I will feel better. More grounded. And then when I wake up, perhaps I will be ready to drive home.

Chapter 24

Amelia

I woke to the scent of coffee drifting through the air, wrapping me up like a warm blanket. The soft sunlight streamed through the gap in the curtains, dancing across the wooden floor. Rich, roasted, too strong. Just how I liked it.

The room, once claustrophobic and heavy with tension, now felt strangely open, like it had exhaled. The tightness in my chest had eased slightly overnight, and for the first time in what felt like forever, a small, genuine smile curled on my lips.

I took a deep breath, letting it anchor me to the moment.

I didn't even remember falling asleep. The last thing I remember was reading Anderson's journal.

The recognition of last night pushed to the forefront of my mind. I looked to the floor where the journal lay upside down, pages bent and flattened. I quickly kicked it under the cabinet beside me as I heard footsteps growing louder behind me.

I took a big stretch to relieve to pain in my back from sleeping in the hard wooden chair.

Lucas appeared from the kitchen, balancing two oversized mugs in his hands, a proud grin stretched across his face. He gave a little half-jog over to me when he realised the mugs were too hot to carry slowly. As I laughed quietly at his expression, he placed one mug in front of me and sat down on the sofa. I grabbed my mug and went to sit beside him.

For a moment, I could have forgotten everything that had happened out here, revelling in Lucas's smile and the cool morning sunrise. Just for a moment.

Lucas stirred his coffee for far too long. Round and round, spoon scraping against ceramic. His eyes weren't on the mug; they were on the trees outside the window.

"You're very happy this morning," I said, eyeing him cautiously while blowing the steam from my drink. When I spoke, he smiled too quickly, too wide. As if the conversation were an echo he was trying to follow rather than lead.

"I guess I am," he replied, still beaming. The smile was genuine, unfiltered.

"And what brought about such a dramatic turn of events?" I asked, my tone light and teasing, but my eyes searched his face for any sign of forced cheer.

Lucas carefully cradled his mug, thoughtful for a moment. "I guess…a good night's sleep," he said. "My head doesn't hurt that much anymore, and the sun's out."

"For now," I said, chuckling softly. At this rate, no one could trust the weather to remain consistent. "I'm glad to hear you're feeling better."

"Yeah," Lucas nodded. "I slept like a baby. No tapping. No nightmares. That's gotta be a good sign, right?"

I sipped my coffee and exhaled slowly.

That is a positive, I thought.

And we're one step closer to going home.

As we prepared for the day, Lucas stood by the window, his gaze fixed on the trees swaying gently in the breeze.

"What time did Jackson say he was coming again?" he asked, not turning to face me.

"I don't think he gave a time. He said he'd call when he was on his way." I fished my phone from my pocket and tapped the screen, checking the volume. I wasn't going to miss that call. The sooner he arrived, the sooner we could leave. Still, I had no signal. I went to ask Lucas to check his phone to see if he could reach any signal, but I stopped myself. I didn't want him to panic if he didn't, I didn't want to ruin his mood.

I walked over to stand beside Lucas. The morning light shimmered through the leaves, casting delicate shadows across the wooden floor. The wind whispered through the grass, making everything feel fresh, almost sacred.

It really is beautiful up here. If only it could stay this way.

"Do you remember the route we took when we found the torch?" Lucas asked, still staring out at the trees.

His voice was light. Too light. Almost absent.

I looked up. He hadn't blinked in a while. Not since I'd walked in. His posture was stiff, like he'd been standing that way for a long time. Too long.

"I… don't think so," I intoned. "Do you?"

A pause. Just long enough to feel like a skipped heartbeat.

"No. I don't think so either," he said.

But he didn't turn to look at me. Didn't smile. He didn't nod as he usually would.

I noticed then. His hand was twitching ever so slightly. Like his fingers were trying to remember something.

"You okay?" I asked.

"Better than ever," he replied too quickly. And then added, like a reflex, "Sun's out."

I forced a smile, but something in my stomach pinched. Lucas was still smiling. He hadn't stopped.

A beat too long.

My eyes narrowed. Something was off. The way his tone had shifted, how he hadn't moved an inch from the window. Why would he lie about the path? And if he was lying, what an odd thing to lie about.

I swallowed my unease. "Why don't we pack? That way, after Jackson gets here, we can just go." I pulled myself up and headed towards the bedroom.

"Why don't we go find the path again?" Lucas said suddenly. "The one where I found the torch. That way, when he arrives, we'll be ready."

I froze in my tracks. My skin prickled cold, and a faint ringing began in my ears. It wasn't the question he asked that made me feel strange. The question itself seemed pretty logical. To someone who hadn't experienced his behaviour in the woods, anyway. It was his *tone* that made my blood run cold. It was monotone. *Rehearsed.* Like I was listening to someone with no acting skills read a monologue. There was no life in his voice.

I blinked hard, trying to shake the unease clawing at my ribs. Maybe it was just the tension. The cabin. The memories. Maybe I was the one who was slipping. I forced a smile.

"Sure. Yeah…makes sense."

I turned to look at Lucas. He hadn't moved; his gaze remained fixed on something beyond the window.

What was he looking at? Why was he acting so… off?

Or maybe this place had just made me paranoid.

I tried to shake off the feeling and headed into the bedroom to pack. Although the ringing in my ears continued.

I wanted to believe it was just stress. The cabin, the isolation, the forest. But the way he'd smiled…too wide, too even. It reminded me of something I couldn't quite place. Like a puppet. No, not a puppet. A mask. A mask pretending to be him. Like someone or *something* was wearing his skin.

My mind returned to what I had read in the journal last night. Anderson said he was leaving. Did he leave? Or did something happen?

My skin itched with the need to pick up the journal and check if there were any more entries. I had to know. But I didn't want Lucas to see it. I didn't want him to realise someone else had heard and seen what he claimed to. Not because I wasn't worried about him, because I was. And not because I didn't believe him, because I think I was starting to. But because I didn't need him to freak out more than he already was.

I placed my packed bag by the door, ready to grab it and go as soon as I could. I laced up my boots, hands trembling slightly. Lucas was already outside, jumper and boots on, pacing the porch with that too-bright smile plastered across his face.

Why was he in such a rush?

"Ready?" he asked, voice light and his eyes sparkling like a child on Christmas morning.

I nodded, mirroring the smile, though I could feel it didn't quite reach my eyes.

As we headed towards the forest, the breeze picked up, circling around us, almost as though the weather were taunting me. Warning me. The twigs and leaves crunched beneath my boots as I entered the trees. Damp and mouldy bark wafted around me, mixed with the scent of decaying leaves and mud. A pit formed in my stomach, and tears began to sting my eyes. A voice circled my mind, deep down somewhere in my subconscious, telling me to run, to go home.

We walked in silence, weaving between the towering trees. The light filtered through the branches in shifting patterns, golden and sacred. It was breathtakingly beautiful. Calm.

Why did I feel so uneasy?

It was quiet. Too quiet. The birds were silent, and the wind welcomed them in waves.

The eerie silence between us made my stomach churn.

236

I kept up close behind him, watching the way he moved. Calm, deliberate, purposeful.

Does he know where he's going?

"What did you say?" he asked suddenly.

"I didn't say anything," I replied, frowning. Had I?

Lucas blinked slowly. "Thought I heard something." He tilted his head to the side as if listening to a voice only he could hear.

"You seem different today," I said carefully. "Not just rested. It's like something's, well, just different."

Lucas didn't answer right away. He looked down at the forest floor. "Maybe I just needed to get out of the cabin."

"Out of the cabin or… back to where you found the torch?" I asked.

He smiled. "Both."

Oddly, the words echoed in the trees.

Feeling unnerved by the unease, I needed to change the subject quickly. Tears welled in my eyes, threatening to spill. My stomach twisted with anxiety. I just wanted my Lucas. Normal, happy Lucas. I wanted my best friend back.

The trees stood unnaturally still, holding their breath. The light that filtered down wasn't warm, it was brittle, fractured. I could hear every shift of my boots on the leaf litter, but not a single birdcall. No rustle of animals. Even the wind moved strangely, brushing the back of my neck like fingers instead of air.

"I want to talk about the other night," I said, finally breaking the quiet that had grown unbearable. I thought that bringing this up might bring him back to normal, make him look at me again. And I didn't really know what else to talk about.

"…Which part?" Lucas asked, his voice unreadable.

"The kiss."

He slowed. "What about it?"

Leaves shifted above, but there was no wind. A hush fell over the trees. Not silence, but something deeper. Expectant. The path narrowed, though we hadn't strayed. A faint hum buzzed in my ear, then vanished when I turned my head. Even the air tasted different. Metallic, like blood on the tip of a bitten tongue.

"I think I was wrong," I admitted. My cheeks flushed with heat, and I twirled a strand of hair between my fingers.

"I know, you made that clear. It was a mistake," he said, his tone seemingly darker than before.

"No," I said, grabbing his hand to make him slow down. "I was scared. I shut it down too fast. Not because I didn't want it… but because I didn't know how to feel."

Stopping and turning toward me, Lucas lifted my face with his fingers to make me look at him. When I met his gaze, his big blue eyes were gleaming like a pool of diamonds. They were mesmerising. I couldn't look away.

"Do you mean that?" he asked, his eyes sharp and unwavering.

He was saying the right words. Using the same voice. But it was as if someone had recorded Lucas and hit play. All intonation, no emotion.

I wasn't sure if this was the best time to have this conversation, but I needed to get him to focus back on me. Take his focus away from whatever obsessed him about those trees. Anxiety bubbled through my veins. I didn't know what to say, but this felt right. And it was the truth.

"I do," I whispered. "I've wanted to do that since the day we met."

The wind stirred around us, whispering through the trees like an audience leaning in. Golden leaves danced in the air. Lucas cupped my face with both hands. Eyes sharp, unreadable, and yet so familiar.

I hesitated. Just a flicker. A breath.

Was this real?

His lips found mine. Soft, then firmer. My body responded before my mind could catch up. It was warm. It was right.

A tremor ran through me. I kissed him back, but a voice pressed in. The same voice that had whispered at the cabin door. *Something's wrong.*

But his arms were around me. He felt safe. He felt like Lucas.

Except his heartbeat was too steady.

Except for the way the rain started all at once, felt choreographed. Not natural.

Still, I sank into the kiss, holding tighter, chasing the version of him I used to know. My mind screamed at me to pull away. My heart begged me to stay.

I kissed him anyway, desperate to believe this was still real. That the boy I met at Uni, the one who used to sketch my portrait on napkins at lunch, was still under this skin.

When we finally broke apart, I was breathless. Dizzy. Unsure if it was from the kiss, or the panic clawing at my ribs.

A crack of thunder rolled across the sky, splitting the silence like a scream. We broke apart, foreheads pressed together, breathing each other in, laughing at the absurdity of it all.

I smiled. "That was…"

"Incredible," Lucas finished for me.

Another boom of thunder. The rain thickened, soaking through our clothes. My wet hair clung to my cheeks, but I didn't care. I could stay in this moment forever.

But Lucas had stilled.

His eyes scanned the trees, narrowed, focused.

"Lucas?" I asked. "What's wrong?"

A pit formed in my stomach, and my heart rate rose. *Not again.* He can't do this to me again.

"Don't you hear that?" he whispered.

My smile faded. "Hear what?"

He didn't respond, just stared into the woods, eyes wide with recognition. The laughter had drained from his face.

Heavier rain began to fall.

The wind screamed.

The trees observed silently.

Lucas took a step forward but didn't blink. He didn't even breathe. He just stepped forward as if someone, or *something*, had just called his name.

Chapter 25

Lucas

All I could hear was the faint, echoey call drifting through the wind. It was beautiful. Melodic. I couldn't focus on anything else.

The voice was there. It beckoned me.

The wind howled, rain pelting my skin, but I barely noticed. My soaked clothes clung to me, leeching heat. But I didn't shiver. I didn't feel cold.

All I cared about was that voice.

"Lucas?" Amelia's voice cut through the wind, tugging on the arm of my jumper. "What do you hear?"

I barely registered her. Her voice wasn't the one calling me. It didn't matter. I shook off her grip and headed up the slope toward the sound.

What was it saying?

I didn't know. But I needed to find out.

I picked up the pace, feet slipping in the slick earth. My breath came heavily.

I needed to get closer.

I needed to hear it properly.

Amelia's voice faded behind me as she shouted my name. Guilt pulled at me from somewhere far down inside my mind. Rationally, from somewhere buried deep inside me, I knew I needed to turn back for Amelia. Deep down, I *wanted* to. But that voice, it beckoned me. It pulled me towards it in a way I couldn't control. I didn't turn back. I didn't *want* to anymore. I couldn't want to. The voice… it was beautiful, familiar.

I remembered her humming in the kitchen. Or was it just the wind? I couldn't be sure. But I clung to it anyway, the way a drowning man clings to debris.

I knew that voice now. It was my mother's.

I steadied my steps, though I didn't need to. I knew exactly where I was going. The voice guided me. It was inside me. A magnetic pull in my chest.

I couldn't stop it even if I tried.

The tone of her voice shifted mid-sentence, like an old, damaged recording. Warping. Distorting.

I paid no attention. I needed to get to her voice. To her.

The sky blackened as I climbed. Thunder growled above. The sun had vanished the moment the voice had called for me.

Lightning cracked in the sky, illuminating the forest just enough to see the trees parting.

I was close. So, so close.

242

I didn't care about the mud slicking my boots or the wind that cut across my skin.

All I could feel was the call.

The forest was opening for me.

And then, an arm yanked me backward.

I slipped, crashing onto the wet earth with a sickening *thud*. Mud filled my mouth. Rage burst from my chest. She was stopping me.

I looked up to see Amelia. Soaked, flushed, wild-eyed. She reached for me again.

I snarled.

"What are you playing at?" I roared, my voice cracking with fury. It wasn't *my* voice anymore. It was louder. Harsher.

Amelia flinched but stood her ground. "What are *you* doing?" she screamed, eyes wide with fear. "What is it? What can you hear?"

"I heard *her!*" I bellowed. "And I'm not losing her again. Not for you!"

The words left my lips, venomous. Unrecognisable. They weren't mine. I barely knew what I was saying.

The rage was not mine. It came from somewhere deeper, darker.

It had taken me.

"It's not your mum, Lucas!" Amelia shouted back, matching my volume. Her voice cracked with emotion. Her face streaked with rain, or were those tears?

"Lucas, look at me!" she shouted, shaking my arm so hard it should've hurt. But my skin didn't register it. She was too warm. Too loud. Wrong.

She sounded like Amelia. She *was* Amelia. But the voice behind her, the other voice, told me she was wrong. It was whispering now. Calmer. Closer.

"Yes it is!" I shrieked. "Get off me!" I tore myself free from her.

"No, it isn't!" she cried. "Your mum's dead, Lucas!"

The scream that left me was inhuman.

"Screw you!" I shouted and shoved her with everything I had.

She tumbled backward, mud dragging her body down the slope. She screamed, the sound echoing through the trees. Raw, panicked, and hurt.

I didn't stop. I didn't look back.

I walked straight through the parting trees.

Time stretched strangely. Each step forward felt like it took minutes. The trees blurred at the edges of my vision, their trunks too tall, their branches too wide. The forest felt bigger than before, or I had become smaller. Or both.

The voice still called. A lullaby in the storm.

My mother's voice.

I pushed through the trees, heart pounding. Not from exertion, but from something deeper. The voice wasn't speaking in words anymore, just sensation. A small flurry of feathers flew overhead, hoping from branch to branch next to me as I made my way further uphill. I glanced up. The small robin danced through the trees above me. A warmth in my chest. A cradle of comfort so seductive it made me forget why I was afraid.

She's here.

My feet moved faster, slipping, catching, scrambling for footing. Mud sucked at my boots like hands, trying to hold me back. I didn't care. Something inside me stretched forward, reaching. Like I'd already left my body behind.

Movement began beside me, rustling leaves and twigs. I glanced down, half noticing the movement, half not caring.

Rats.

Tens, maybe hundreds, of rats. All scurrying beside me along up the pathway.

I knew where they were leading me.

The forest opened around me, but it wasn't a natural clearing. It felt... intentional. The trees thinned too evenly. The canopy above stopped swaying; wind caught in some unseen breath. Everything was holding still.

Fog coiled at my feet like something alive, tendrils sliding between my ankles. It moved without wind. Not drifting, but slinking.

Amelia's voice was still calling behind me, but it sounded far away. Like a television in another room. Wrong channel. Wrong life.

The birds had stopped. The trees didn't creak. No branches snapped beneath my boots anymore. It was as if the forest had made room for me. Cleared a path to the altar.

A soft hum rose from the ground, or maybe from the back of my skull. It vibrated in my ribs. The lake wasn't visible yet, but I knew — *knew* — it was near. I could smell it. Wet moss, iron, something faintly sweet.

The world felt... quieter.

Not peaceful. Expectant.

The closer I got, the calmer I became. My pulse slowed. The chill in my fingertips faded. I felt… anchored.

This is what I've been waiting for. I'm finally where I'm supposed to be.

The voice was fainter now, not gone, just softer. Like it was waiting.

I turned in a slow circle, scanning the treeline.

"Mum?" I whispered. My own voice felt too loud.

There was no one there.

Then, my eyes fell on the lake.

It lay ahead of me, stretched wide and still like obsidian glass. A mirror without flaw.

It hadn't looked like that before. Had it?

The rats disappeared into their crevasse. The lake pulsated in response. It was welcoming them.

The surface shimmered faintly, as if something below it was breathing. A faint pulse, a ripple, that didn't match the rhythm of the rain or wind. It moved independently. Alive. I whipped my head to my left, where the sound of moving twigs came from. The robin perched on a small branch of the closest tree, head cocked to the side. Watching me. I don't know why, but its presence calmed me.

A bolt of lightning cracked overhead. The clouds split open for a heartbeat, casting a strange, violet-yellow flash across the surface.

The lake caught the light and changed.

Colours bloomed. Not natural ones. Lavender, bruised blue, rose-pink and ink-black, swirling together like spilled oil. Hypnotic. Artificial. Dreamlike.

I allowed the pathway of tulips to guide me forward, and the scent hit me. Not tulips, not water, not rain. It smelled of old lavender perfume. Soap. Warm laundry.

My mother.

I dropped to my knees, eyes wide. The lake had become a lens. I could see something in it. Not just a reflection, but a scene. Or the memory of one. My childhood bedroom, flickering. A hallway. The worn sweater my mum used to wear on Sundays. Then the image dissolved. My breath stilled. I couldn't move even if I tried. I didn't want to. The ripples slowed. And then, the voice. Right behind my ear. Just one word. Whispered.

"Lucas."

I flinched, but no one was there. Only the water. Only myself staring back. My reflection shimmered into view, blooming in the centre of the lake like a painting appearing on wet glass.

My own face. But something was off. I leaned in and stared into the water. It was captivating.

I blinked. My lungs burned, but I hadn't noticed I'd stopped breathing. A soundless exhale left me as I stepped forward, drawn by a force I couldn't name. The forest behind me no longer existed. There was only this place. This quiet. This calling.

Then… a shadow.

The black grew larger, darker as it began to engulf the colours. Still, I felt at peace. Safe.

I heard Amelia's voice behind me. Distant and frantic. I ignored her. The world hushed around me. My mother's hum was louder now. Closer. The pinks and purples faded. The water stilled. Blackness took over. The surface rippled, not with wind, but breath. Slow, measured. It was breathing. For me. Its surface bubbled until all my eyes could focus on in this obsidian mirror was my own reflection.

My name hummed through the mist. Not a whisper. A note, low and vibrating, like it was coming from inside my own lungs. It echoed through my bones. I stared into the black water. It stared back. The figure mirrored my position exactly, but the face... the face was off. Subtle things first: the eyes blinked too slowly, too deliberately. The pupils were too large. The smile was too... present.

It began to move without me.

I didn't move, but my reflection twisted its head.

It raised one hand.

My arms stayed limp at my sides.

Then the reflection smiled. An awful, twisting thing that bent and stretched the mouth too far, exposing teeth that were too many, too sharp.

Needle-like.

My chest tightened. My instincts screamed, but my legs wouldn't listen. I was frozen. Not by fear, but through allure. There was a pull deep in my gut, a promise of something. Wholeness. Reunion. Relief.

The reflection mouthed something. No sound, just lips moving. *Come closer.*

In this, I realised, maybe the bird we saw when we arrived here was dead. The rabbit too. And after seeing this, a real-life reflection of myself staring back at me, I realised maybe a part of me was dead as well. A part that the forest feasted on, consumed in its entirety. Brought here to face me. Show me that not all that's gone is lost. I could be whole again. If maybe I just got a little closer…

The reflection's eyes grew, ballooning with madness.

My throat closed. Panic flooded in.

Reality consumed me, and I scrambled backward, slipping in the mud.

I wanted to move. I had to move. But I wasn't sure which way was which anymore.

"Amelia!" I tried to scream, but the wind swallowed the word.

My phone fell out of my pocket, hitting the ground with a crack. I tried to crawl to it with all of my strength, but it had skidded away into the dark.

Too late.

The surface of the lake erupted in a deafening explosion of soundless violence.

My reflection *launched* from the water, solid and soaked, like a corpse tearing free from the grave.

Its claws, no, fingers stretched into claws, stabbed into my abdomen. Curling like blades beneath my skin. The crack of my ribs echoed through the clearing.

I screamed. High. Animal.

The reflection didn't flinch.

It grinned.

Slick, skeletal hands tore into my side, peeling away flesh with surgical ease. I watched in horror as a slab of meat, a part of my body, was flung into the water. It sank without a ripple.

Warmth flooded my shirt, then turned cold. Rain mixed with blood and soil. My breath hitched as my intestines uncoiled, steaming in the air like broken cables. My stomach collapsed inward.

My body spasmed.

One leg kicked violently; the other twitched once and stilled.

The thing dragged me forward, closer to the water's edge.

I tried to claw backwards, but my nails only raked through sludge. The strength left my limbs as if it had been drained, sucked out of me by the thing's grip.

My eyes rolled, chest heaving as panic strangled my throat.

The creature tilted its head and leaned in, impossibly close. Its face hovered inches above mine. Eyes swollen, unblinking, unrecognisable.

Its mouth *unhinged.*

Wide.

Wider.

Too wide.

Joints cracked. The jaw detached with a wet pop as if something had dissolved the tendons.

Rows of teeth unfolded, not like a shark, but like a deep-sea parasite. Endless and serrated.

Then it bit.

Glass-like teeth punched into my neck.

Crunch.

The world spun.

The last thing I saw was my own body being pulled under the surface.

250

The water rippled.

Then stilled.

Chapter 26

Amelia

Excruciating pain pulsed through my wrist and shot up my arm like fire under my skin. I couldn't move, not yet. When my head finally stopped spinning, I opened my eyes.

The world spun around me in a fog of greens and browns. I was lying in thick, clinging mud, soaked through my clothes, scattered with debris and sharp twigs pressing into my skin. Rain poured down in heavy sheets, not washing the mud off, but blending with it. Coating my body in a wet, suffocating film. My wrist throbbed viciously, unlike any pain I'd felt before. It was fractured, maybe shattered.

My head pounded. Dull at first, then splitting. I must've hit it in the fall.

I touched the part of my skull where the pain resonated from. A warm, sticky liquid oozed from a gash in my hairline. I winced at the pain of my touch. I brought my hand down into my vision, careful not to move my head and make the throbbing worse. Red coated my hand, dripping between my fingers and snaking its way down my wrist. I gagged, bile burning up my throat, sour and acidic. It stung my cracked lips, mixing with the dirt already crusting my face. I wiped my mouth with my sleeve, but it only smeared more muck across my skin. The world tilted again, black spots dancing at the corners of my vision.

I stayed on the ground, eyes shut tight, letting the rain slap my face like punishment, like maybe it could wash away what just happened. But it didn't.

The pressured ache moved from the top of my head down to behind my eyes.

The memory didn't knock; it hit me like a brick. Lucas. His face twisted in rage. The madness was in his voice. The push.

The slope.

Where was he now?

I forced my eyes open, half-expecting to see him hovering above, shouting my name in panic. But there was only the sky. The trees. The storm. He wasn't there. Not even a distant silhouette. The emptiness screamed louder than the wind. A halo of light formed in the middle of my vision; I had the thumping pain to thank. I tried to blink it away and failed. Covering my eyes with the palms of my hands, I tried to steady the spinning in my head.

Had he even looked back and seen me fall?

Had he even cared?

I tried to sit up, using my wrist on instinct. The moment I did, white-hot agony shot through me, tearing a scream from my throat. My stomach lurched, and bile climbed up my throat. I clutched my wrist to my chest, sobbing. Deep, helpless sobs shook my entire body.

What is happening?

He looked at me as if he didn't know who I was. Like I was something crawling out of the trees. That couldn't be Lucas, not my Lucas. He used to bring me coffee in the mornings. He used to hum when he got nervous. The boy I loved wouldn't shove me. He wouldn't leave me.

I reached into my jumper with my good arm, frantically patting myself down. No phone. It must have fallen. Maybe it was shattered somewhere on the slope.

I was alone. In pain. Trapped in this nightmare.

Still crying, I dragged myself upright using twisted branches and sodden roots, my broken wrist cradled tightly against me. Every movement felt like torture. The trees seemed to press closer. The wind screamed like grief in my ears.

"Lucas!" I cried, voice hoarse, cracking with desperation.

No reply. Just shrieking wind. The groan of branches. The thunder rumbled far off.

He left me.

He really left me.

Had I misread him the entire time? Had I missed the signs?

No, it wasn't real. It couldn't be. Maybe he slipped. Maybe I misheard him. He wouldn't shove me, not Lucas. Not the boy who had just kissed me.

I forced myself to move, sliding one foot forward, then the other. Mud sucked at my boots. I slipped, then recovered. Again and again. My vision blurred from rain and tears alike, my head still throbbing. My breath came fast and shallow, my chest tightening with panic.

"Lucas!" I screamed again, louder now. More rage in it. More betrayal.

How could he do this to me?

Tears poured hotly down my cheeks, indistinguishable from the rain.

Hatred and love.

Confusion and fear.

It all tangled inside me. Every step was agony. I could barely see. I had no idea where I was going, only up. Up, toward where he'd gone.

I had to find him.

The trees seemed to lean in, their branches whispering secrets too quiet to hear.

A sudden gust slammed into me, stealing my balance. I stumbled and instinctively reached for a branch with my bad hand.

A sickening *crack*.

A scream ripped from my throat. It echoed through the trees, swallowed quickly by the wind.

My body convulsed with pain. Tears streamed freely. My vision narrowed, my head dizzy. I fell back on my knees, pain consuming me. I couldn't swallow it down this time. My stomach emptied onto the sludge beneath me, mixing with soggy mud and leaves, sliding down the path and covering my hands and knees.

The wind moaned, low and throaty, almost forming words. The trees creaked not in time with the breeze, but like bones adjusting after a long sleep. I glanced left. For a moment, I thought I saw movement. A shape ducked behind a trunk, but it was gone before I could blink.

I put my head in my hand, sobbing from the pain, the sickness, the situation. Rain poured over me. I wished it would wash away the sadness and the hurt. It just washed the sickening mixture further over my body.

What is going on?

I stood barely. The wind whipped in every direction. My clothes clung to me like wet paper. The forest roared and howled, a storm of its own fury. I pressed on anyway.

Every root became a threat, every step a negotiation with pain. My vision pulsed, dark at the edges, tunnelling forward.

I saw Lucas laughing on our first hike. That crooked grin, the crinkle in his eyes. I'd kissed him under these same trees. Had that even happened? Had it all been part of the illusion?

The forest didn't answer. It only whispered to the wind. And still, I climbed. Hands raw, knees slicked in mud, heart fracturing with each footstep. I wasn't chasing hope anymore; was chasing the *truth*.

"Lucas!" I cried again, voice ragged. It was a plea now. My final one. I was at the edge of collapse.

Then, silence.

The wind slowed. Like someone turning a dial. Just a soft whistle now. The rain softened but did not stop. Even the sun had peaked back around the clouds to view the aftermath of what it had hidden from. I hiccupped a breath trying to steady myself. My mind not being able to comprehend what was happening.

A distant creak echoed through the trees. Not the sharp snap of a branch, but something deeper. Slower. Like wood shifting after a long

slumber. I turned in place. Nothing moved. But the trees seemed...
closer. They leaned in, their branches craning, listening.

And then, was that a voice?

A faint scream in the distance. Male. Agonised.

My blood turned cold.

Was that him?

Or just the wind again?

I reached the top of the slope and saw the trees part ahead. A circular clearing of land opened before me, surrounded by gnarled trunks like watchful eyes.

I staggered forward.

It was eerily still now. No wind. No birds. The trees stood, holding their breath.

And there, glinting on the ground, something metallic.

I blinked hard, trying to make sense of the clearing in front of me. My brain had disconnected, like the shapes weren't real. A phone couldn't just lie there like that, in the centre of such stillness.

The light above me didn't flicker, but the shadows did. The trees weren't swaying, yet they seemed to move.

I crouched, barely breathing, reaching out with fingers that didn't feel like mine. The metal was warm. Or was it? I couldn't trust anything anymore.

It was Lucas's phone.

Blood splattered across the screen; it was still wet. Still red. Still fresh.

I stared, unmoving.

The world muted.

258

Every colour dulled. Every sound muffled.

Even the wind had stopped. The forest had heard enough.

My fingers tingled. My throat went dry.

My brain screamed at me to move, to run, to scream. But my body wouldn't respond.

Then I heard it. My name.

Distant. Behind me.

But I didn't turn around. I was rooted in place.

I just stared at the blood.

Lucas.

What had he done?

I dropped the phone and collapsed into the mud, shaking with uncontrollable sobs. My scream came out strangled and weak.

"Lucas!" I howled, my voice cracking under the weight of grief and fear. "Lucas!"

This couldn't be how it ended. Not like this.

My hands dug into the mud, my nails scraping furrows through moss and rot. The sound that escaped me wasn't even a sob, it was a shuddering, gasping plea for the world to *stop*.

"Why?" I croaked. "Why would you leave me?"

But the trees offered no answer

I curled into myself, holding my broken wrist and crying until my lungs gave out. My body convulsed with each breath. The pain in my bones was nothing compared to the agony splitting my heart in two.

"Amelia?"

The voice was real.

I looked up through tear-soaked lashes and saw two shapes approaching from the parting in the trees. Jackson. And another officer.

Their faces morphed from confusion to horror as they took in the sight of me.

I was a wreck. Mud-soaked, arm bent unnaturally, clutching my blood-covered body. Screaming silently. My head thundered with agony. I wasn't sure if it was the physical pain or the realisation that my world would never be the same again.

"What happened?" Jackson asked, almost tripping as he rushed to me, skidding in the muck.

I didn't answer. I couldn't.

I couldn't form words.

Jackson's voice was too loud, too sharp against the hush that had swallowed the clearing. He didn't belong here. None of them did. I flinched as he approached, my mind still trapped in the moment where Lucas shoved me away. A man like that couldn't exist in the same world as this uniform.

I just sobbed harder into my palms.

Jackson dropped to his knees and wrapped his arms around me, trying to comfort me as best he could.

His partner was already radioing back for help.

Jackson looked at the phone in front of me. "Is this his? Is it Lucas's?"

I didn't respond.

"We've got to get you out of here. You need a hospital," he said gently, glancing at my wrist.

260

I didn't care about the pain. Only the void.

He gently lifted me to my feet, and I let him. Like a doll, limbs slack, head bowed.

"Where's Lucas?" he asked again.

I just cried harder. I couldn't say it. Couldn't speak aloud.

Because to say it might make it real.

Jackson squeezed me tighter as I nearly lost my footing again.

Together, we started moving. Back through the opening in the trees. Step by step. Just before we reached the slope, I turned. One last glance.

And through the mud, the mist, and my blurred vision. I could have sworn I saw it. A shimmering circle. Water, where no water was before. Where no water should be.

A lake.

A rippling reflection stared back at me from the heart of the forest.

The surface throbbed. Not with wind, but movement. Something beneath the waterline shifted. A single tear slipped down my cheek as the fog crept back in, obscuring it from view. And for a second, just a second, I thought I saw a figure standing at the water's edge.

Epilogue

It had been a year to the day since it had happened.   After P.C. Jackson had found me in the forest's clearing, he took me straight to an ambulance that was waiting for me by the cabin. I spent three days in the hospital with a fractured wrist and what the doctors referred to as *acute psychological trauma*. My parents had come to join me, staying by my side and helping me with my recovery. They went on all the searches for Lucas in those woods, and there were a lot of them. Anderson's sister flew over to help look. More so to look for her brother, I suspected, but she still came. But me? I couldn't bring myself to set one foot back in that forest.

The police questioned me intensely. I was, after all, the last person to see Lucas. I'd been found with his phone next to me. Blood splattered across the screen. I knew what it must have looked like. But no matter how many times they asked, all I could speak about was *the lake*. I begged them to search it. I *knew* he was in there.

But they never found a lake.

P.C. Jackson and his partner swore there was no such clearing. No such water.

Still, the damage was done.

I was sectioned just days later. Three months in a psychiatric facility.

My parents admitted me. I didn't blame them. Not anymore, anyway. I wouldn't stop talking about Lucas, the reflection he had seen in the window, the tapping at the glass, the lake. I screamed in the night, clawing at the walls and sobbing that something was still out there. Eventually, my parents had given in to the fear that I was unwell. They thought it was their only option.

And it was.

For three months I'd sat with my thoughts trapped inside the walls of my mind, and of the hospital.

The mirrors were always covered, a precaution after I screamed at my own reflection. I'd insisted it had blinked when I hadn't.

The nurses gave me soft food, soft voices, soft restraints. Nothing sharp, nothing real.

And every night, I heard the tapping.

I'd stopped telling the staff after the third time.

They'd forced me to speak to therapist after therapist. I could tell that some of them thought I was hiding something. That I knew more. That I had *done something.* Others were more convinced I was simply broken. Psychotic and delusional.

But one therapist, just one, offered something different.

He suggested that what I saw might not have been literal. That it could be a form of deep trauma response.

He told me of children who had invented monsters, aliens, ghosts, anything their minds could make sense of, because reality had

264

become too horrible to process. Their brains protected them from the truth with stories.

Could that really be what *my* brain had done?

"Sometimes our minds bend the truth just enough to survive it," he'd said, tapping the arm of his chair in an oddly familiar rhythm. "Doesn't mean it didn't feel real."

But how could something feel real and not be? I didn't believe in ghosts. But I believed in what I saw.

No.

I knew better. I had been there.

I had seen Lucas change, heard the tapping, and even seen the lake. I remembered how it had shimmered like glass. How it *changed* him. But I also knew that if I agreed with the therapist, if I nodded along and pretended, I would get out faster.

So, I nodded. I lied.

And I was released.

I never found out what truly happened to Lucas. No one did. But deep down, I knew he was gone. He wasn't coming back. Not Lucas, not Anderson. And I knew it had something to do with that lake.

I promised myself I would *never* return to that place.

Now, I sat in my rusted red Beetle at the bottom of the uneven path that led through the trees and back to the cabin. My hands trembled slightly on the steering wheel. I'd gotten my licence after leaving the hospital; it was the first taste of freedom I'd had in months. My parents tried to smother me after everything. Understandably. But

I needed to feel something that resembled living. I need to feel like I wasn't trapped.

I had dropped out of Uni when I returned from the facility. Couldn't focus. Couldn't pretend. But I joined a charity. One that worked with families of missing people. Through that work, I found my purpose again. A small, quiet purpose.

When I told them I planned to visit the site of Lucas's disappearance on its anniversary, they'd said I was insane. They knew the whole story.

Maybe I was insane. But it felt right. It felt necessary.

I turned off the engine and leaned back in my seat, sighing. My leather chair creaked beneath me. I glanced at the old map folded beside my gear stick and traced the route with a trembling finger. But the lake wasn't marked. It never had been.

I lit a cigarette. A bad habit, a guilty vice, but the only one that dulled the pain even slightly. Smoke curled from my lips and drifted out the cracked window. The scent of earth, bark, and memory lingered on the breeze.

The forest should have scared me. But it didn't. And that was the scariest part.

I hadn't expected it, but it was almost… comforting.

The scent of damp wood and rosemary. The sun warmed my cheeks. The pinks and purples of wildflowers danced across the forest's distant grass. It was like seeing a long-lost friend.

I reached over and picked up the bouquet from the passenger seat, cradling them in my lap for a moment.

I checked the rearview mirror. Not looking for cars, there wouldn't be any, but for myself. The reflection that stared back looked like me but weathered. Older. Eyes rimmed with the kind of heaviness that sleep never fixes.

A breeze nudged through the open crack in my window. It didn't carry fear, not yet, but something else. Curiosity. Memory. I took one last breath, flicked my cigarette out the window, and opened the door.

The warmth of the sun welcomed me like a soft blanket. It felt like the first actual sunlight I had felt all year.

For a moment, I smiled.

But even as I smiled, something tugged beneath my ribs. A kind of hollowness. Was I really ready for this? I had spent a year convincing myself I could forget, that I could fold the past neatly into memory and lock it away. But driving here had peeled open something raw.

What am I hoping to find?

Forgiveness? Closure? Or something worse?

I approached the beginning of the pathway and paused. The trees were the same. So tall. So still. But the sickening eeriness slithered up my spine. The hairs on my arms stood on end. I remembered Lucas's smile. How he looked at me just before it all went wrong. Just before he disappeared.

I remembered the kiss. So tender, so passionate, so real.

Tears burned in my eyes at the memory. I still loved him; I would always love him.

I squeezed the flowers tighter and stepped forward.

The trees whispered above me, not in language but something older, something knotted into the bark and roots.

I could almost hear his laugh behind me. The quick, breathy one he used when something genuinely caught him off guard.

Each step forward felt like pushing against an invisible tide, one thick with regret.

I had told him about the emails. I was the one who suggested we came here.

I remembered the last proper laugh we'd shared before all of this, before the cabin. He'd spilled energy drink down his sleeve and pretended to cry about it on the drive up. I'd snapped a photo. It was still saved somewhere in my iCloud.

He came only because he loved me.

And maybe, deep down, I knew I had wanted him to come here with me.

That was the worst part.

I hadn't told him I loved him. Not then. Not when it would've mattered. I remembered sitting in the passenger seat, watching the trees blur past the window, too afraid to reach for his hand.

He came only because he loved me.

The thought clawed its way to the forefront of my mind again, and I winced.

The guilt choked me. And yet, I kept walking.

I could almost hear his footsteps behind me. Always too quick, always offbeat, like his mind was three steps ahead of his body. He used to hum songs without knowing the lyrics, making them up as he went along. I used to tease him about it.

I remembered how he'd stop every few minutes to comment on the moss, or a funny-shaped rock, or the tree that looked like a question mark. That was Lucas. Curious, distracted, and endlessly kind.

The trees seemed to lean in, listening. The moss clung to my boots like hands. A root curled upward, almost tripping me, reaching for my ankle.

Eventually, I found a flat patch of grass just outside the trailhead. I knelt there and laid the bouquet of tulips gently at the base of a crooked tree. The bark was mottled with moss and age. I traced my fingers across it as if it were an old gravestone.

"I'm so sorry," I whispered into the wind.

"I miss you."

The words broke me. Tears bled down my cheeks, hot and helpless. I laid my head against my knees and let them fall freely, sobbing in the arms of the forest.

The breeze stilled. Even the trees seemed to brace themselves.

A crow took flight from a nearby branch, shrieking into the silence.

Then everything went too quiet. My pulse beat against my throat. I could hear it. I could hear *everything*. The shifting bark, the stretch of roots, the slow scrape of something unseen just beyond the trees. The calm before the storm.

Then everything started again.

The wind howled through the trees, dead leaves whispered along the ground. It was as if the forest were reacting to me. *With* me. They were comforting to me. And then, something else. A sound. A whisper. A voice.

Lucas?

I froze. The wind roared again, but beneath it I could have sworn I heard my name. Faint. Echoing. Calling me.

My breath caught in my throat. My skin prickled with the dread I thought I'd buried. I turned my head slowly toward the trees. The trees didn't stand still. Not really. I was sure one had shifted or leaned closer. Roots writhed just below the moss, like something sleeping fitfully.

The wind rose again, carrying whispers that brushed past my ear and dissolved before they became real.

The shadows shifted.

The leaves rustled.

The forest *breathed.*

And again. Soft, broken, *close-*

"Amelia…"

My heart stopped.

The bouquet tipped from where I'd placed it. The petals scattered across the ground.

A single drop of water slid down from one of the flowers, like a tear.

I stood.

The thick blanket of grey cloud had appeared in the sky as if from nowhere, blocking the sun's gaze. The wind whipped around me, causing my hair to move in a frenzy.

I tugged my hair away from my eyes and investigated the treeline. Rain erupted from the sky with a crash of golden light. It lit the path in front of me as if it were an invitation. A welcoming. A small robin sat perched on a branch at the forests entrance, almost of if it were welcoming me.

Instinctively, I began twirling a wild strand of hair between my fingers. I could have sworn I could see something just beyond the trees. Just ahead, by the edge of the path. With his hoodie pulled up, smiling that crooked grin I knew so well.

I stepped forward.

He vanished.

A trick of the mist. Or not.

Then, faintly: "You'll be bald if you keep twirling your hair, Mills…"

My knees buckled. No one else called me that. No one else could. That voice, it was his. But slightly too slow. Slightly wrong tone. A cold prickle flushed my skin. My limbs were stiff, they were frozen. They weren't mine anymore. My fingers tingled as if they were falling asleep. My lips felt dry, though I hadn't stopped breathing. My body, now as numb as I felt inside.

My feet moved before my thoughts did.

Closer to the trees. Closer to the shadows.

My name whispered again.

And somewhere in the distance, beyond the edge of logic, just past the veil of memory and madness —

The lake shimmered.

And something smiled.

Acknowledgements

Writing a book is a strange mix of obsession, discipline, and questioning every life choice you've ever made. I couldn't have done it without the people who kept me going throughout the process.

First, to my mum, who not only supported me from the very beginning but bravely read my first draft without once questioning whether I was going insane. To my sister, Cherisse, for reading chapters as I wrote them and cheering me on even when I doubted every word. And to my dad, whose encouragement arrived exactly when I needed it.

A huge thank you to my friend Amber, who read my second draft, helped me edit, and gently pointed out the things I absolutely needed to fix (even when I pretended I didn't). You made this book better in ways you'll never fully realise.

To my husband, thank you for the endless support, the patience, and for pretending not to notice when I disappeared into my laptop for hours. You kept me sane, or at least as close to sane as a horror writer can reasonably be expected to be.

To every poor person who sat near me whilst I asked, "Have I spelt this right?" for the hundredth time… I'm sorry. Truly. Your suffering was not in vain. And with every *minuet* that went by, we *defiantly* learnt how to spell things correctly.

To my dogs, who dragged me out of the house for fresh air and walks when I would've happily fused with my desk chair. You have no idea how much of this book you're responsible for.

To my incredible ARC readers and my brilliant editor — thank you for stepping into the shadows with me. Your sharp eyes and honest thoughts have helped shape this book into something far stronger than I could have created alone. You've caught the things that hid from me between the lines after hours of re-reding. I'm endlessly grateful for you.

And finally, to you, the reader. Thank you for picking up this book, for giving it a chance, and for giving me the encouragement to keep going. Your support means more than you know, and it's the reason I'm already writing the next one.

About the author

I'm Chelsea Knight, an author from Essex, England, though my imagination tends to wander far beyond that. I've always been drawn to the darker corners of storytelling. The quiet dread, the subtle supernatural, the things you sense before you see. As a kid, I would always try to convince my parents that I was absolutely old enough to watch horror films and read scary books. I wasn't. The nightmares proved that *(that damn Scooby-doo)*. But the obsession stuck.

Before I ever thought I'd write a novel, I studied Animal Science BSc (Hons) at university, then trained as a primary school teacher. Eventually, I traded lesson plans for something a little more chaotic: running leisure businesses, bars, and nightclubs with my husband. Somewhere between designing escape rooms and managing late-night crowds, I realised I had a story idea that was too unsettling to build into a physical escape room, but too good to let go. So, I wrote it instead. That idea became *Dead Things Grow Here*, my debut novel.

I write because I love it, because my head is full of strange little ideas that refuse to stay quiet, and because there's something addictive about exploring the line between reality and the uncanny. I'm inspired by authors like T. Kingfisher, Dot Hutchison, James Herbert, and anyone brave enough to blend horror with heart (or a touch of dark romance, of course).

When I'm not writing, you'll usually find me walking my two dogs, where most of my best ideas ambush me. I also love reading, lifting things at the gym, and drawing or painting whenever my brain needs a different kind of creative chaos.

Dead Things Grow Here is my first step into the world of publishing, and I can't wait to share more of the stories that have been haunting me for years.

Connect with me:

Tiktok and Instagram: @chelseawriteshorror

Email: chelseaknightauthor@gmail.com

Where The Dark Glows

Out in Autumn 2026

Chapter 1

Georgia

The moment my foot hit the dock, the water rippled like it was breathing. A gust of wind swept across the harbour, stinging my already reddened cheeks. I bit down on my lip, the salt air and a metallic tang mixed in my mouth. A fishing boat clanged somewhere behind me, its ropes knocking against the mast in an uneven rhythm that made my heart rate rise. A whisper of voices became swallowed by the wind that whipped around me. I turned to see where they came from, but the pier was empty. Just the sea stretching out in each direction, dark and endless, as if the world simply stopped beyond the horizon. The wood creaked beneath my feet, loud enough to expose the panic I was trying to swallow. I clenched my jaw to stop myself from blurting out that I didn't want to go with them. I couldn't go. I'd spent the entire morning trying to convince myself that today would be fine. That I wasn't six years old anymore. That the ocean wouldn't hurt me the same way again. But fear doesn't care how old you are, I guess. And the closer I got to the end of the pier, toward the ocean, the more it seemed like the tide remembered me, too. With each footstep, the water swirled around the wooden posts beneath me. The deck groaned lengthily and deeply under my weight, sounding almost spiteful. As the boards vibrated, a subtle tremor travelled up my legs. Not enough to be alarming, but enough to make me pause. To make me wonder if the dock reacted to me, not the waves. Nico's cousin's speedboat bobbed at the extremity of the short pier. Its chipped paint, frayed ropes and rust growing up its side didn't build my confidence. The kind of vessel that looked like it had many stories to tell, none of which I wanted to hear.

Liam stood on top, his shaggy blonde hair blowing in the wind as he put his foot up on the stern, mimicking a pirate looking through a spyglass. Nico quickly joined in, jumping onto the boat in the typical 'Nico' way. His exaggerated movements and his loud "Aye, M'Heartys" echoed across the ocean as he threw his arm over Liam's shoulder and cheered their half-drunk beer cans together. The boat tilted side to side with more vigour at each of their movements in a way that made my stomach turn. Amara's melodic, and almost forced, laugh echoed over Nico's showboating as she walked towards them. She held her perfectly curled hair down from the wind in one hand and was live-streaming from her phone in the other. I watched as they all messed about, teasing each other and hyping each other up for what was about to come. However, my thoughts drifted.

My gaze was locked onto the water. It rippled as if something stirred just below the surface. My eyes glazed over and I swallowed down the acid that rose in my throat. I recalled the last time I had been in the ocean. It wasn't a memory I wanted to return to, but fifteen years didn't diminish what I felt each time I remembered what had happened. The shock of the cold water swallowing me whole. The muffled roar of the sea filling my ears. The way the sunlight fractured into broken shards above me, unreachable and fading fast. The panic. My arms flailing as the current dragged me deeper. Someone had screamed my name. I never found out who that was…

Sweat beaded on my forehead as my gaze tunnelled deeper into the water as if it were about to show me what lay beneath. The wind curled around me, too deliberate to be natural, as though it expected me to fall. Waiting for me to make a mistake. Liam's voice broke through my thoughts, bringing my attention to the stinging in my eyes.

"Come on, Georgia!" he called over to me.

His voice seemed kind and full of excitement for the adventure Nico had promised us. I wanted to call back and tell them to go on without me. That I would wait for them in the hotel; finish the book I've been meaning to finish all weekend. The wind picked up, sending shivers up my arms as I pulled the sleeves of my jumper down to cover more of them.

"Georgia!" he called again, waving his arm, beckoning me towards him.

The glistening sparkle in his eyes made my stomach twinge for a different reason now. My nerves briefly turned to excitement. Not to go on the boat and into my nightmare, but to spend time with the guy that made my cheeks flush just by a sideways glance. Liam studied me for a moment, his brow tightening. I took a deep breath. The salty air mixed with diesel as Nico set on the engine. *I can do this,* I told myself. The wind shifted suddenly, brushing the back of my neck like a cold fingertip. I took one more glance at the blackness beneath me before finally nodding and continuing down the dock towards them. The wood creaked and rocked with each onward movement. I kept my eyes fixed on Liam. If anything happened, I had him to look out for me. He's brave, and he wouldn't let anything bad happen, I hoped. If I was protected with Liam anywhere, it was near the water.

A board beneath my feet crunched and dropped an inch as I got closer to the boat. I stopped, frozen in the explosion that had erupted in my chest. Liam jumped out the boat and jogged over to me. My cheeks grew hotter and the thought of him thinking that I was scared. Of course, I was. But I didn't want him to know that. A low hum vibrated through the dock, too steady to be the tide, almost too distant to be the boat's engine. It groaned like something beneath us was waking up.

"Hey," he said, his tone gentler than before. His hand rested on my arm, my knees buckling under the weight of his grip on me.

"Are you okay?" Genuine concern filled his eyes as his grip tightened on my shoulder. My head felt dizzy; I blinked, trying to steady myself.

"Yeah, sorry. I… I get seasick," I confessed. Technically, that wasn't a lie. He relaxed his hold on me, resting his hand on my back instead.

"We don't have to go if you don't want to. I mean it,"

The offer hit me harder than it should have. The water rippled beneath the deck again, and my chest tightened.

"No," I blurted. "I'm fine."

A lie, but one I needed to believe.

"It'll be okay," he flashed me a smile that, in any other circumstance, would have caused my entire face to blush.

But right now, his deep dimples were no match for the darkness churning just below my feet. If he believed I could do this, maybe it was true. I swallowed down another bout of nausea and gave him a faint nod. He guided me towards the boat that loomed just a few more feet ahead. As I stepped closer, the boat drifted toward the dock with a slow, deliberate glide. The hull tapped the wood once. Twice. A third time, harder. Liam didn't seem to notice.

Nico still jumped around the boat, yet to have calmed down his childish excitement. Liam called out to him to calm it down for a moment whilst I got on the boat, steadying me by the arm and helping me up.

"Come on, G, it's not like the sea's gonna eat you," Nico laughed.

An icy shiver crawled down my spine, sharp and instinctive.

"Don't say that," I whispered before I could stop myself.

"Come on. It's Cornwall, not the Bermuda Triangle." Nico said.

"Same energy," Amara muttered, applying another layer of lip gloss to her already shiny lips.

Liam snorted. "Be nice."

"I am nice," Nico said. "I'm the nicest one here."

Amara rolled her eyes. "You once pushed your cousin off a jetty because he said you were getting chubby."

"I'm not chubby!" Nico said, offended.

Their bickering should've relaxed me. It usually did. It was normally funny. But today, every sound was too sharp. Too loud. Nico rolled his eyes at Amara and welcomed me by tossing me a beer. My foggy mind wouldn't register it quickly enough as the can slid through my shaking hands and thudded on the ground. It twisted side to side, a small hole in the top shooting out beer like a punctured vein. Nico ran towards me, jolting the boat violently as I instinctively grabbed Liam's biceps to steady myself. My death grip wouldn't relinquish as Nico dove to the floor by my feet, grabbing the can and latching his mouth over the split top. He squeezed the can until he had downed its contents, crumpling the can in his hand and throwing it into the ocean. He glanced towards Liam, and then at me, shrugging.

"No wastage!" he laughed, hitting Liam playfully on the arm as he made his way back over towards his girlfriend.

Amara sat on the bench along to edge of the boat, moving her body and angling her phone to get the correct lighting for the best selfie. After hitting ten thousand followers, her phone became an extension of herself, and being near her gave the impression of being in the Big Brother house. She documented everything, posted everything, and more often than not, she livestreamed her life to her followers. I had learnt to be careful what I said around her, not wanting the world to know my secrets. I hoped she wouldn't be livestreaming when I inevitably threw up over the edge. She stayed so engrossed in making herself appear the best in her selfie that she didn't even notice

Nico bounding towards her like an excitable golden retriever. He made it over to her, grabbing her in his arms, scattering little kisses all over her head and face. Her other hand reached out and grabbed the phone he almost had flung out of her hand and overboard. She scrunched her face up, trying to push him off her. Liam let out a soft laugh next to me, clearly finding her irritation amusing. His eyes locked with mine, his hand brushing a stray strand of hair from my face as the wind picked up again. My body froze. I couldn't smile back or say anything; I was completely caught in his gaze.

The boat jolted forward. My body lurched, hitting the middle seats and sliding to the floor with a thud. I pulled myself up to my knees, my heartbeat thumping in my ears, my clammy hands trying to pull myself back to my feet. My eyes darted around the boat, trying to make sense of what had just happened. Liam sat on the floor, rubbing his head, his eyes moving quickly around us. Amara's face scrunched into a ball as she ran her fingers through her long black hair. She was muttering something under her breath, trying to tame her locks from the sudden assault of wind. Nico stood by the wheel, a huge grin plastered on his face.

"Let's go!" he howled. His voice seemed to echo over the ocean while the boat moved forward. Too fast for my liking.

I continued to get to my feet. My legs were unsteady beneath me. Staggering to the boat's side, I held on for dear life. I sat myself down and latched onto the pole around the edge as the boat leapt over the waves. Fog had started to come in thick at the horizon, bringing the end of the ocean closer. The sky dimmed so gradually that I almost didn't notice. A low rumble vibrated through the air, like a throaty growl.

Amara lowered her phone. "Did you hear that?"

"Hear what?" Nico shouted over the engine.

Another vibration rolled beneath us, rattling the metal frame of the boat.

Liam frowned, glancing back at the water. "Probably just the engine."

But the engine hadn't made that sound before. The sound had come from underneath us. The fog closed in, edging close like a door to a cage. My breath came sharp and short as my claustrophobia clawed its way in. The sea air drowned me. For a moment, I tasted saltwater again. Cold, metallic, and wrong. The memory struck me. It slammed into me so hard my knuckles whitened with my grip on the railing. I focused my gaze on the water, the thick black liquid foaming at the edge of each wave. Something dark drifted beneath the water. It moved fast, chasing us through its own path. The more I stared at it, the darker it became. As if it didn't want me to see it, just wanted me to know it was there, watching me. The tide pulled sideways, unnaturally, as if the sea itself attempted to get away from us. Trying to escape the assault of the speedboat that ripped through the sea. The darkness chased us across the ocean, tossing us over each wave. Fog chased us, stalking us, almost engulfing the eerie horizon in its murkiness. The clouds followed, looming overhead, a dull slate-grey that pressed against the horizon. Air blew ice-cold against my skin as we tried to outrun the inevitable. The rain came next, thumping down onto the boat's hood, crashing against the waves. It hammered on the boat, each impact sharp and jarring, as if the sky had cracked open. It went through me like gunshots to the centre of my brain. I tried to focus on one thing, the shadow lurking just below us, but everything was starting to become too much. The fog, the loud heavy rain, the salt air that wrapped itself around my airways and sat heavy in my chest. A faint buzzing sound filled my ears, soft at first, then rising until it drowned everything else out. The world tilted. Suddenly, I was at peace. Everything paused. It felt as though I was finally able to breathe freely. The fog gave me space, the rain generously failed to make a sound, the waves stopped – steady and still.

And then, a crash.

It snapped me out of the brief haze, my silent moment of peace in this nightmarish venture.

Something brushed the underside of the boat.

I froze.

Another smack.

Then a long scrape, like nails dragging across the hull. The boat jolted frontward again and then stopped. My body flung forward, my hands slipped off the wet railings as I tumbled to the floor. My head cracked against something hard, and then… darkness.